THE POWER AND THE GLORY
AND OTHER LESBIAN STORIES

THE POWER AND THE GLORY
AND OTHER LESBIAN STORIES
Collected by Miriam Saphira

Papers Inc.
Auckland
New Zealand

Published by Papers Inc., P.O. Box 47-398, Auckland, New Zealand.

Cover Design   Miriam Saphira & Romi
Typeset by   West Plaza Copy Centre
Printed by   The Print Centre, Auckland

ISBN 0-908780-40-0

CONTENTS

Siggy

PREFACE

I am an avid collector of lesbian fiction, lesbian non-fiction, lesbian magazines and lesbian dinner party invitations. I have run out of book shelves, filing boxes and my clothes do not fit me any more. All of this makes me feel good. Also I am a dreamer. One day I thought if I have dreams, ideas and ramblings then I felt sure other New Zealand lesbians would have them too. From time to time some of us write them down as short stories so it seemed a good idea to share these with each other.

This collection is not big but it offers a glimpse of our thoughts and ideas before they are lost with the memories of barbeques at Raglan, parties at Trafalgar Street and custody battles in High Courts.

These stories are a beginning. They break away from stereotypes and bring our struggles, our loves and our humour on to the page. I hope that our readers will have as much pleasure from The Power and The Glory and Other Lesbian Stories as our collective has in putting it together.

— Miriam Saphira

Dedicated to those lesbians who paved our path.

Robin Adams

I was born in Auckland in 1933 and educated at Northcote College. I tried various jobs, such as, landgirl, then trained as a librarian. I worked for one year in Fiji and three in London. I have done some travelling but less than I had planned. In 1979 I was forced to retire through ill-health. Now I have time for carving and the things that before, I didn't have time for. I was closeted until mid 1986 but I now feel the need to be as honest as possible without embarrassing my family. My 23 year old relationship broke up three years ago.

I love walking, sailing, the outdoors and am a compulsive book buyer and reader. Also, I could not live without a cat.

The Well of Loneliness

This verse was written in 1954 when lesbianism was still considered deviant and sick. Everyone was so closeted that each thought she was the only one who had these "disgusting desires". The isolation and loneliness was of an intensity that would shock the luckier, young lesbians of today.

These two poems remind us of our beginnings and make a story in themselves.

Alone and tired,
Tired and afraid,
Afraid to live
but not afraid to die.
Young in body -
And yet so old in strife,
My very youth
A bitter laugh at life.
Is there no peace?
In death is peace,
A peace I've never known
In life.
A man shall reap
As he has sown.

What bitter sowing this
What stunted seed
Produced this life?
What thought, O God, what need?
Is there a God?
God made you what you are.
Drink deep of the Well
In your own mind is Hell.

For Gwenyth

Nature goddess? Earth mother?
You are elemental woman.
You vibrate with Earth's rhythms,
Making me vibrate in unison.
The spring seems more fecund for your presence,
The autumn more fruitful.
You bring to the swing of the seasons
Understanding that helps me too, to understand.
Through your eyes I see -
Through your ears hear.
Let me worship at your altar.
You are woman
You ARE.

Fran Marno

I was born in 1946 and spent my childhood around dam sites in Mangakino. I came out of marriages into feminism and innumerable women's workshops and groups a few years ago. I'm a lesbian, artist, exploratory writer, and mother of two daughters.

The Beginning of it All

It's pissing down with rain and Jo and her mower are sloshing and singing around my back garden. She gets paid twelve dollars for churning up the ground out there and I get this crazy witch woman (she spells it "womyn, eliminates the male") stuffing her sodden pockets with feijoas. She educates me on tin roofs (like mine) that keep the spirits out. There's no way I can afford to re-roof.

It's her lover that I know. Vickie used to work with my husband. He propositioned her once. That was before he'd known she had a woman lover and after he'd propositioned the two other women he worked with. Vickie told him to keep his high-intellect slime at home, which didn't please me too much as at the time I happened to be that 'home' and his regular tension release. Vickie and Jo eventually met me. I had been duly educated, instructed and given a high-powered theoretical rundown by my husband on how to relate to lesbians. As far as I knew I hadn't met any before. I remember thinking "next week I'll be thirty six. I've got one dead husband, two kids, one new husband who wants other women and blames me when he can't get them and two lovers who complain to me about their wives. Now I'm about to meet a 'lesbian couple'. Life back here in New Zealand is looking up."

Today, Jo stands solid in her dripping khaki shorts and clinging t-shirt chewing some flower stem she's taken a fancy to in my back garden.

"Love mowing in the rain — amazing atmosphere down there — your oak tree's a real matriarch — she's magic."

I wonder if Jo talks to her other lawn owners like this. She's had her mowing round for six months now and I know her more than I do Vickie. I seldom ever see Vickie.

Jo swallows the chewed stem with apparent ease and produces one of her intense looks.

"Vickie and I are splitting up."

Every couple I know is splitting up, separating, letting go. My husband and I have. I don't like her telling me this. I don't want lesbians to split up. I don't know why. I've never given it a moment's thought. I just know I don't like it.

"Why?" I ask lamely.

She's sitting on the couch on a towel, rolling a joint. She sucks in hard and coughs the smoke out.

"I fell in love with a witch."

I hope my eyes register suitable approval. I'm choking on my disbelief.
"Oh?"

"You've met her. She was at our place the night you came round for a drink."
She was too.

"I've been in love with her for three weeks — Magic — we can connect even when we're in different cities. Vickie's told me to move out."

Women stay together for life. Lesbians are different. Jo can't leave Vickie. I've left lots of men, and some have left me, but it's not the same. I'm not going to discuss it. I just know.

"Thought I'd like to build myself a living space in your basement. Think about it."

I think about it. Not about her. Not about Jo and Vickie. Downstairs is full of large junk. It's dark, dusty and probably damp too. It was a workshop when my husband was in his carpenter phase. I hadn't admired his talent enough so it had become the children's club hut. Now it's crammed with things my husband wouldn't throw out. Things he wouldn't take with him when he left.

"No problem. It's a disaster area but if you want it, fine."

"Thanks." She sounds sincere. I don't think she wants to leave Vickie.

"And how do you feel about having a wild dyke downstairs?" (Lesbian is the word my husband used. He would slip it into conversations "they're a lesbian couple" or "Liz and Anne? Well, I imagine they're probably lesbians." It was very 'in' to be an aware supporter of minorities.)

I like Jo saying dyke. It's somehow more intimate. My husband would never have used it. I can't say it myself — well — not without sounding self-conscious.

Jo's laughing. I light a cigarette. I'm nervous of exposing my relationships with men to her. She's met them: my ex-husband, my lover, my flatmate. She likes my lover. "It's all there" she's told me "he's just a bit off centre."

This is quite different though. She's not used to having men around. I am. I'm a very good listener; they like that. I don't threaten them (well not intentionally). I let them do their thing and I do mine. It's a placid household. I don't want that to change. I'm scared it might.

"I'm really happy for you to have downstairs Jo." I'm trying to smile, to appear welcoming. "It's just that, well, this house is full of men. I didn't think you'd like that."

"I've thought about it. I can handle it. Might even broaden their horizons."

"Maybe." I doubt it.

Jo stands up. She stands with her feet apart, hands pushed into her damp pockets. "Some day this will be a women's place. I can feel it. Good vibes."

I'm not really ready to visualise my house and garden swarming with lesbians. I suppose she does mean lesbians when she says women. I very seldom think about the future. Still, I'm relieved that she's picked up good vibes. I feel somehow included in her vision. I'm a little bit flattered.

"There'll be streams of dykes visiting me downstairs." I wonder what my household will think. I wonder what my neighbours will think. Will they know; be able to guess?

"Could be a few witches flying past your window this summer." She looks out at the oak tree. So do I. "I'll be sitting under her when the moon's full — she's beautiful."

I smile weakly. I hope I look enthusiastic.

"Be over with my crowbar and my mattress in a few days" she tells me. "Chow — and thanks."

Jo pulls on her heavy mud-laden mowing boots. She strides out into the rain, extracts her drenched mower from the dripping overhangs, heaves it deftly onto the truck and drives out of my life for two weeks.

Fran Marno

Ngahuia Te Awekotuku

I am a Maori scholar who loves chocolate and cats, and writes academic papers and lesbian stories.

Whero . . . three pieces, starting early

Ha! Your titties are smaller than mine are!

No they're not! Anyway, I don't care. You're just being stupid.

The bathwater rippled and flickered, catching black shadows cast by the stubby candle squatting in its chipped enamel holder.

Wild shapes danced on the mossy, damp walls, softened by decades of rising steam. Whero stretched her short, flea-bitten legs. By chance, her toes, the nails jagged, touched the slim brown flank of her cousin Heni, long and luminous beneath the gentle waiariki. A strong fist grabbed her ankle.

Gotcha!

Hey, Heni, stoppit, eh! Lemme go!

Nope. Not till you soap my back like you promised.

Oh, all right. Where's the soap?

I dunno. You gotta find it, kiddo. Ha ha!

Four young seeking hands groped about the sandy bottom of the mineral spring, following the length of old wooden slats, sunken in the mud; exploring carefully the concrete slabs and seating.

And they always found more than just the soap. 'Cos Whero and Heni, once in the bath, always stirred up a good time, learning a lot, laughing a whole lot more. Heni, so much wiser — her breasts so full and firm, her hair so black and crinkly. She drove her little cousin mad; she loved it. Heni, with gold flecks in her eyes, and a brown spot in the white of one. Heni, sturdy poi-girl wrists, and flashing wolf teeth, and the ancient, ageless knowing of one who had "done it already."

But Whero didn't want to know; she didn't need to. She just wanted Heni, she knew that much. But she couldn't keep her.

The bath-time touches and teases were only that. Only teases.

And Whero's brother Jimmy got her instead.

After all, he was a man.

And wasn't Heni a *real* woman?

15

Whero is sixteen, and she feels *good*. Her supple young fingers knead and smooth and rub the scented oil into the pinkly pitted buttocks; looks around the room one more time, taking in the black ceiling and navy blue walls, the sheep skins scattered on the kauri floor, the freckle-dusted body an apricot stretch across the huge, cloudy bed. Merlene. The mother of one of the kids in her class at school. She played Bach and Thelonius Monk on her hi-fi, and she introduced Whero to the pakeha custom of drinking a real Tom Collins from a highball glass. Wearing a lilac gown of transparent silky stuff she lit curly candles everywhere, and burned incense sticks, and revealed her soft golden stomach with a smiling, smarmy pride, See, I'm not even a Maori, but I'm darker down here than any of you lot. I sunbathe whenever I can, even in July. Yoga in the sun. Just a few minutes a day, that's all it takes. What d'you think, Whero?

Whero was beyond thinking anything. Her Saturday nights out were not to the pictures with her mates, as her mother thought, but to this weird room, and even weirder woman.

Who soon got sick of her.

And then the word was out. One of the teachers found out about Merlene, and teenagers (not just young girls, either), and the hi-fi and the incense sticks, and the Tom Collinses in highball glasses.

So Whero pedalled home in the wee hours of the morning, her finger tips aglow with Merlene's sighs. Cautiously, quietly, she slipped her bike into the shed. Steam rose silent from the garden around her. She started looking for her cat.

Whero! Where the hell have you been?!

Oh Mum! You gave me a fright! I —

You've been with that Johnson woman, haven't you! Haven't you!

Oh — Mum, I was just —

I know you have! What are you? What is she? A bloody lesbian, or something?!!!

WHACK!

Two years later, and in the Big City. Alone, the only Maori girl in a formidable university hostel. The only Maori girl, that is, who wasn't a maid or a kitchen hand. One of them, Tia, was from home, and she'd been around. She knew everything about everything in this huge bloody ugly place. Even where the *lesbians* were.

At the Ca d'Oro. Pot of gold, neon light spilling onto the slick, wet city street. Whero sat in a corner, blue jeans and red skivvie and old tartan swandri; waiting for them to come in. She fiddled with the mini juke box machine on the wall — 'Guantanamera" — soothing strokes, Merlene. And through the door they came.

Shane. Rickey. Ant.

Royal blue beatle suit and lush white, frilled shirt. Hair the colour of spangled gold; and beautiful, deep, dark brown eyes. Ant. So tiny, muscular, tight. She drove TQ midgets at Western Springs, and was training to be a mechanic. Yet her hands — long, tapered, graceful fingers — were soft, flawlessly clean, and strong. The handshake was electric. But she was on with Rickey. One massive butch, who was the size of a ten ton truck. And Whero was stunned. By Ant. Blown away. Hopeless. Bewitched. In love. Crazy. Desperate. Pleading. What was she going to do?

Set things up with Shane, to get to Ant, away from Rickey.

A passionate, pitiful kind of loving — confined to feverish clutching in the bog at the ferry buildings; under the lifeboats on the Kyoto Maru; behind closed lavatory doors at Gleeson's pub.

Theirs was simply not to be — not then, not ever. Rickey was always alert, and worse, she got heavy. And Ant was lured away by the femme charms of Trina, irresistible, a whiter shade of pale. Trina, who was a fashion model, fancied Ant in beatle boots, flapped her glossy false eyelashes, and announced she was AC-DC. So what the hell. How could Whero possibly compete with someone like that?

She wouldn't dare.

Fran Marno

Nicola Patterson

My Mother

My mother wanted me to stop writing nonsense. She tried to rescue me from infinity and I was rescued by her many times at costs far greater to herself than I was then ever to know. The price and the reason was love. I burned through however, with love and condemnation for the world I was to fit within — I was not to fit within it. Everything smeared itself in my direction. At adolescence I couldn't cope. I, her child at adolescence, but by the time the future came and she had rescued me one more time too many, the cost of all her rescues (of me) paid its price on her. She was tired. She had coped too much. Her rewards were minimal. She tried too long, she had struggled.

And now I fortified by her great love faced infinity alone and took intrepid footsteps within its bounds and my mother perceiving this and my non need for rescuing, my defiance towards the end of tomorrow sighed: you are lesbian, she said for all her sources that she sought of past experience and learnings said to her: no this is wrong, this is dangerous, this is abnormal, this is *gross*, can you rescue your daughter from this and her daughter's memories and her own memories sliced into one another and her mother stretched herself into infinity's shadow this time and saw darkness. Daughter, daughter I can not speak anymore and she thought to herself:

for I have loved you truely,

and she hung up the phone

and was deeply hurt

not understanding

Not understanding not understanding and her daughter, who was I, who am I breathed breath then tainted by the poison of generations of learning and oppression that asked too much of her mother and tainted and burdened her mother with too much. And her mother took on every burden unquestioningly in purity far purer than should be asked ever of any, but yet asked in our oppression of all women without asking or acknowledging merely expected, my mother had taken on all this and succeeded more brilliantly and successfully and beautifully than any had ever seen.

And now the breath I breathe, that I love, that is pure, that my mother rescued me for many times has been cast in dark shadows, so dark that the very light by which I, her daughter, see loses my mother within them. She, churning out dark shadows forever cannot churn out this one and cannot understand and the irony of time's time breathes itself upon us.

For how can I say that my mother in rescuing me endlessly has given me this, that her life will not allow her to have or even perceive? Now I feel strong and clear. I am lesbian and I acknowledge all it means with awe, and my mother breathes backwards, now gently, into the past and cries. She is lost and alone in shadows she has rescued me from and from which I cannot rescue her.

Siggy

Aorewa McLeod

I was born in Auckland in 1940 and have lived here all my life, with odd periods overseas. I have been a dyke since I was 21, with odd short regressions into heterosexuality. I have taught English Literature for 17 years and have been a closet writer for three years.

In The Park

This summer every park seemed to be full of drunks: men in frayed dirt-hardened dark suits, sitting on the park benches with the open bottles in brown paper bags on the gravel under them, or resting against their sides. Their faces and hands were burnt a dark red-brown — a distinctive sunburnt colour that was quite different from that of the farmers back home or the golden tans of the English wealthy and the tourists.

No-one ever sat on the same benches with them and they were always alone, or very occasionally in a silent pair sharing a bottle. They all looked aging — their stubble was always gray against the strange ochre skin. But it was a very distinctive sort of aging too — they didn't look like other old men. Like Down's Syndrome children they all looked alike, as though they shared a chromosome difference or belonged to a different race.

She found herself studying them with a secretive fascination as she walked slowly through the Squares, on her way to the British Museum. They'd be there at 10 am; and still there at seven in the warm summer evenings. They looked so alike it took a while for her to realise that they must circulate: that they were not the same ones who'd been there a few hours earlier. Yet they never seemed to move, except sometimes to lie down on the bench or under it.

And increasingly she began seeing the women. Were there more women among them, or was she just noticing them now? The women's clothes, like the men's, were dark, frayed, stiff with dirt, but often their legs were bare under their skirts, and they too were stained the same deep brick-red against the worn-down cracked black shoes. She winced at the thought of what feet would feel like, cramped naked in that hard darkness.

Where did they go at night? she wondered. Had they ever had lovers, husbands, children?

She drank at home, alone, sitting on the small hard sofa or lying on the bed reading. But the bottle beside her on the floor, its open neck protruding from its brown paper bag was the same. What would it take to turn her into one of those women? Or how long? Each evening, walking home, the bottle's weight heavy and comfortable in her shoulder bag, she watched them.

At night she dreamt of her mother. In her dreams the ground stirred, her mother's hands reached groping towards her out of the crumbling grey soil of the grave and she would start running. She fled panicking: knowing that she would be captured and brought to trial for her mother's murder: knowing that her mother had kept some strands of her hair and some nail-clippings, and had cast a spell on her: knowing that her mother would capture her and that that dead embrace would be horrible, and the end.

Waking, she knew that her mother had been cremated, that it had been many years ago, in another country, on the other side of the world. But sleeping, her mother's corpse pursued her. She slept badly, often waking in the dead quiet hours of the early morning, and pouring herself another drink to help her sleep again. It was a basement flat — she would walk out into the small walled garden, glass in hand, and sip it staring up at the dull red glow of the London sky.

One day she drank a couple of cans of barley wine in the ladies loo at the British Museum. That was not so unusual in itself, she often drank there now, saying to herself — "well, that's about as low as you can go, drinking in the toilets." But the toilets at the B.M. didn't seem to belong to the outside world. They were like toilets everywhere; enclosed hidden cubicles in rows, painted identical toilet colours. Secretive places where nobody looked or spoke to anybody else, walking quickly to their own single space, peeing as silently and crapping as sweetly as possible, and looking in the mirrors only at themselves, never at the person behind or next to them. The Museum library was always so full of people, none of whom she knew. And behind the vast halls of the Museum itself, full of enormous dark Assyrian Gods and lacquered enigmatically smiling Egyptian Queen-Goddesses; behind the blank white flanks and faces of the Elgin Marbles, were the toilets — toilets that were identical to the toilets in any public building anywhere.

She had been sitting at her desk, reading the novels of a woman dead years ago and thinking yearningly of the enclosed cubicle and the cans in the shoulder bag at her feet. She waited for the hour she'd allotted herself before leaving her books and papers. But this time, after drinking them, pulling the tabs as she flushed the loo so no-one would hear the hiss of escaping froth, she didn't go back to her desk (P.Q.11, two-thirds of the way round the vast dome). Instead, smiling goodbye at the silent guards at the entrance she walked through the gate of black and gold and out into the sunlight and across to Russell Square. First though, she had to go to Monmouth Street where the nearest off-licence was. Then, back walking slowly into the Square, eyes half closed against the brightness of mid-day. The lawns were a lurid English green and the beds were full of ranked orderly summer flowers. She went down the central gravelled path under the huge elms, towards the cool splashing of the fountain. Yes, they were there, sitting oblivious, each on a separate bench. A race apart.

She sat down on one of the few unoccupied benches, opposite a dozing woman, and watched her. She was fattish, her clothes stained down the front, her overcoat gaping open, tied round with what might once have been a man's tie. Greenish-grey socks hung loosely over soiled sandshoes. She stared at her face: heavy jowls of the familiar dark red-brown above a collection of sack-coloured scarves. The greasy grey hair was pulled back in a tangled pony-tail with a piece of string. The mouth was slightly open.

Her mother's face had been very pale — flabby and white. She rarely went outside except to go to the shops, and in the last years not even that. She, like her daughter after her, drank alone, hidden. After her death it had taken the best part of a morning to clear out the empties from the cupboards, from under the sink, from under the house, even under the bed.

But this woman reminded her of her mother — the same fat grubby untidiness. She crossed over and sat next to her and leaned towards her. There was a hot smell of never-washed clothes and urine.

"Excuse me, but could you tell me why . . . ?" What was it she needed to ask?

". . . Would you mind talking to me a bit?"

The woman's eyes opened, staring at her. She felt the shock go right through her: they were her mother's eyes, pale-blue, looking directly at her out of the face of this drunk in Russell Square. Her mother back from the grave —

"Fuck off — Go on — Piss off . . ."

"I only wanted . . ."

"Fucking, pissing, nosey bitch — Fucking well, piss off — Piss off . . ."

The voice was slurred but loud, and getting louder. She got up hurriedly and pulling the paper-bagged bottle out held it out towards the woman.

"Here, I thought you might like this . . ."

The woman's flailing arm caught it and it hit the gravel with a smash. An aura of port fumes rose around them. They both stared silently at the reddening bag. Then she turned and ran from the Square to the nearby Tube station.

The Cypriot store on the corner of her road was an off-licence so she stopped there, buying a bottle of Greek white wine and another bottle of port. She felt grateful for the shopkeeper's smile and his comment on the lovely day. Back in the dingy light of the flat, pouring the wine over ice-cubes, she wondered what she had wanted to ask the woman and what she could possibly have answered. What was the question? She remembered asking her mother time after time:

"Is anything wrong?"

"No, nothing."

"Can I do anything?"

"No, nothing. I'm alright."

"Have you been drinking?"

"Of course not. Don't be silly."

And she remembered her mother's look of indignant, hurt innocence. Was there an answer?

Later that afternoon she realised that only half the port bottle was left and went out. Not to the Cypriot shop this time: she didn't want them to think she was a drunk, but to the supermarket five minutes up the Holloway road. She put a packet of crumbed turkey steaks in the supermarket basket with the gin and tonic. That way she didn't look so obvious, and besides, she'd better have something to eat.

She tried to read, but the words kept slipping away, so she turned on the TV. She lay on the bed sipping, the bottles propped up in the folds of the duvet, while a programme on Bolivian Indians was followed by one on a rare species of gannet. But all the time she was recalling the woman's face which had now become indistinguishable from her mother's, and imagining scenes where she beat at her with her fists: where she smashed that face in, swung an axe and split her forehead open. The brain crushed and pulped and the blood splattered out. She stamped her back into her grave — stamped on those groping hands, breaking the fingers, grinding them back into the soil. And she was screaming as she stamped:

"You fucking bitch — You bitch — you bitch . . ."

The violence she felt surprised her. Drinking usually filled her with a sentimental good-will. And she hadn't hated her mother, only pitied her — or perhaps despised her. She began crying. God, they must be tears of pure alcohol by now, she thought.

Then she ran and fell on her knees before the toilet bowl, vomiting up a black gush of fragments and fluid, vomiting again and again, unable to stop, vomiting up her mother, the drunk in the park, vomiting up her guts. And she knew, clutching the cold white porcelain, retching up the last slimy pieces, that when she'd rinsed her mouth, washed her flushed face, blown her nose, wiped around the toilet, she'd go back to the bedroom and pour herself another drink.

Siggy

Aorewa McLeod
The Beginning of the Story

How to start? She stared at the page of her exercise-book. Under her neat heading "The Qualities of a Good Poem" she'd jotted down phrases the famous poetess facilitating the group had given them from her bright red lips: "words to make connections" — "the sudden moment of recognition" — "seeing the same familiar thing but transfigured." (Sounds like falling in love, she'd written in a parenthesis to herself.)

Now they sat in silence around a collage of tables — about twenty women — each writing a poem. Each connecting words and words, each committing an act of passion.

She ripped a blank page out of her book. It might be easier to begin if it looked like a casual scrap of paper — to be discarded, not kept and reread. The classroom was bare and stripped. Sanded wooden unvarnished floors with walls of whitey-yellow chipped paint. There were no decorations of any sort. It was as bare as her paper. Except for one crookedly hung painting. Surely that couldn't be the same fifties sort of yachts that she'd stared at through hours of boredom? They couldn't have kept it for thirty-five years? She stared at it. Was this the same classroom she'd sat in thirty-five years earlier? Could it have hung there for thirty-five years? Back in the same schoolrooms and once again asked to write. But now, not asked to write like an adult, but to shed her fifty-two years one by one until she had shed her repressions and restraints, shed the twenty-five years of teaching, the twenty-five years of struggling to get words out of reluctant ballpoints, shed the anxiety and constant sense of failure. The kids hadn't liked her — they'd sensed her tension and her uncertainty as to what it was she wanted of them. They liked the certainty and bad jokes and personal cracks of teachers like Robert Wrigley and Janine Stanton.

Yet, stripping away those years of teaching, what had her sixteen year old self — sitting in this classroom or one like it — possessed that had been repressed or lost? All she could remember was the boredom — the huge monumental unutterable quality of that boredom. It had been so unbearable she could remember her whole body aching with it and yet it had had to be borne. There was no escape.

She could escape now. The woman beside her — Vicky, she thought her name tag had said — had almost half a page filled with large sprawling writing.

26

It looked like a poem but was too illegible for Josie to read as she squinted at it sideways. All she had were the famous poetess's instructions on how to write a poem written tidily at the top of her page. A school teacher's writing she thought glumly — neat, meticulous, well-spaced. Fuck it! She shoved her book and paper back, and muttering "loo" in case they thought she was piking, went out and leaned over the balcony, staring down into the hall below.

The large gilt-framed oil paintings in the school hall were definitely the same ones she'd stared at through years of assemblies — dutifully opening and shutting her mouth to produce a hazy mumble of hymn-like noises. Tall thick kauri trees with peeling silvery bark in Northern forests. Southern blue mountains, their snowy peaks touched by pink sunlight. A dark but discernably defiant stag at bay to snarling dogs. She hadn't seen the paintings for thirty-five years but they were as familiar to her as her own face in the mirror — more so — for they hadn't changed. They stood huge and eternally the same. She stared down at them with loathing, while wondering if the stag painting was meant to convey some sort of message (what?) to adolescent girls.

Underneath, Melinda smoking, leaning against a dirty yellow pillar, lifted her eyes from the fascinated inspection of the oils. She knew every curve of the peeling bark, every detail of the fern fronds of the forest floor. Twenty-five years ago she'd gazed blankly at them while she'd sung and prayed and sat cross-legged. She could still sit cross-legged for long periods — her legs permanently shaped by those five years of morning assemblies. Above her and to the left she watched the woman staring down at the same paintings. She'd seen her before at the novel-writing workshop. A strong face with prominent heavily lidded eyes, an aquiline nose and lots of deep lines. It was the clothes that had struck her though — a mosaic of bright colours — yellow, purple, red, black — dishevelled, untidy even, but striking. An interesting person, a powerful person, she'd thought. Pity she dyes her hair. She'd look great grey.

She found herself looking up into eyes that looked into hers. Embarrassed, she smiled and nodded. The woman smiled back. A grin, thought Melinda, that's what a grin is. She'd been trying to write a poem about faces. All she'd got so far were two lines:

"I ought to have shut you up years ago."

His face snapped shut.

Everyone else had written real poems. She'd known they were real because they bored her and she couldn't hear them. Poetry had always done this to her. And their poems were long. The famous poetess hadn't known what to say about hers. "Have you written some more?" she'd asked. Melinda was feeling pleased she'd read it — though if it hadn't been for Jay prodding her knee saying "Go on — Go on", she'd never have done it. And then bloody Jay had passed. Perhaps she would write about a grin — this grin above her. "Her face stretched open" or "she opened herself" — no, perhaps . . .

"Can I have a cig?" It was Jay — little punk Jay with the blond spiky hair and alert untouched face. Brilliant little Jay, as good with words as she was with paints. "Come on — be good for you" Jay had said. "There'll be plenty of people there who don't write, who haven't had things published." But now she said "Bloody shambles isn't it?"

"What workshops are you going to?"

"I'm taking time out. The one I wanted to go to never happened."

"Funny, I went to school here. That's my name on the honours board."

"Where?"

"There. Melinda Lawson, Head Girl, 1965."

"Head girl eh. You must have been a goody-two-shoes. I was here too. Needn't look for my name though. They'd given up expelling by 1983 or I reckon I would have been expelled. Pissed off that I wouldn't sit for Scholarship. And I don't think that stag at bay's ever recovered from the day-glo spray. My mother was here too. What with me being the daughter of an old girl and her being a secondary teacher and all that, they just kept cautioning me."

Goodness, thought Melinda. I wonder what the mother of a baby-butch like Jay would be like? She imagined someone severe and disapproving, like her teachers of twenty-five years ago.

"Do you get on with your mother?"

Jay grinned. She loved Jay's grin — it was wise and cheeky and toothy. I must write about grins, she thought.

"That's her up there" and she nodded at the woman above, who was now talking to a tall white haired woman. "She's O.K. We get on fine, now I don't live at home. She's neat actually. I keep telling her she'd make a brilliant dyke."

"Funny — I wouldn't have picked her for a school teacher."

"She's not any longer. Got pissed off with it a few years ago. She's not a bad writer actually. I reckon she's going to write New Zealand's second great novel. One day."

"Do she and your father live together?"

Melinda realised she was asking her question very tentatively. "How little I

The Beginning of the Story

know of Jay," she thought. Two years at Art School together, innumerable coffees together, even painting together and she realised she knew nothing of her. And she realised she was disturbed thinking of Jay with a past that had formed her. Jay seemed new born, crisp and clean-cut and self-assured. Tough and talented — how could she ever have had a mother!

"Christ no. There've been a fair few since him. Alexa my older sister — she's in the States doing a doctorate — she's the legal one — the product of the marriage. He went religious — a fundy. Me — my father — he's one of the last of the hippies. Lives in a commune in the Hebrides. A right-disaster area. Him, not the Hebrides. Then there's Ratapu. We still see a fair bit of his Dad and their family. He's got dozens of brothers and sisters and hundreds of aunts and uncles and thousands of cousins. The last guy lasted nine years or so. They broke up a couple of years back. Now, he was one of your liberal left-wing laid-back men. Called himself a feminist and belonged to a men's group. They're all the same though. He tried to get into me after years of positive parenting. I think she worries that it's the men she chose that made me a dyke. But hell — they're just representative. All men are shits."

Jay inhaled deeply and dropped her cigarette on the bare sanded floor and trod on it.

Melinda was half aware Jay was proud of her eccentric fathering. But she was worrying how Lara would describe her mother's marital career by the time she was Jay's age. She thought she'd be pleased if Lara turned out anything like Jay. Not the smoking though.

"Well, I'm off. I know it sounds ageist but I'm tired of workshops run by 50-year-old writers. No offence Mel — at least you're under 40."

"Old enough to be your mother", she said morosely.

But Jay simply grinned, raised her hand in farewell, swung her haversack over her shoulder and left.

I wonder what Jay stands for? Probably Jessica or Jeanine. No. More likely Jocasta or Jezebel with that background. A moment later she saw Jay above. She grinned at her mother, said something, ruffled her wiry hair and vanished.

Josie smoothed her hair, looked after her, and back down at the woman Jay had been talking to. Was she a lesbian too? Far older than Jay's lesbian friends. But she had short hair, and decidedly tat clothes and grubby sneakers. Just then the less well known poet's voice called out on a rising intonation;

"We're going to begin reading back now ladies — so — if you could just . . ."

"I suppose we should go back. Have you written anything?"

"Not a word."

"That's all right then. I'll go back if you will."

So she and the white haired woman, whose name tag unbelievably said Evelyn Murgatroyd, went back. She squeezed into the narrow space next to Vicky. Christ, she was on her second page. Or perhaps it was her third! Closing her eyes Josie thought — it's like falling in love, like a moment of passion. Very fast, without thinking, she wrote words on the ripped page, putting them in lines to look like poetry:

That moment of recognition
Of the connection between word and thing
Between word and word
That moment of passion
(like falling in love she'd added in her notebook)
That moment when you realise —
Is the beginning of the poem
Or of the affair.
That person over there talking
That person is Love.
A tingling in the palms
Hand reaching for a pen, or a body.
A tangle in the chest
A tangle of sea-green growth swelling and choking, blocking the throat,
Till she saw only the line of a shoulder, a gesture —

Christ! That is quite enough! What garbage! As they began reading their poems round the group she tried to focus on the words, not the faces of the women reading them. But today she was obviously into watching, not hearing. The words blurred so she watched the faces. She could see what Jay meant when she'd whispered, leaving, "too mature for me Mum." The youngest'd be the one with the baby in the pram and she'd be well into her thirties. She could feel Vicky's disapproval of her doodling. She hadn't doodled much since she'd been at school, perhaps occasionally at University, and she was amused to notice her doodles hadn't changed. Still outlined profiles of tilt-nosed girls and aquiline nosed gents to whom moustaches and beards were added later. Must be the school atmosphere. Her poem? was surrounded by them up and down the margins of the page and as the time got nearer and nearer to the lunch hour (they had to be on time or the hosts would be offended) the faces began to overlay the poem, till the words, to her relief, vanished under the faces. She

30

noted words that reached her from poems: "I'm sorry" — "the wharf stretched out" — "mushy" — no. "Mushy" was from someone's comment on Jane's poem about leaves — leaves melting into the pavement. "Perhaps they were mushy" the less famous poet said helpfully. "The orange bucket on the stairwell."

"Eyes meeting" she wrote in the interstices of her faces and it was time.

Too many women, too many words. Badly timed. The famous poet had talked too long about herself. Just like the famous novelist last night. So after twenty minutes they had to stop.

After a long wait sitting on benches watching the girls perform their poi dances and sing their waiata they filed in to an enormous lunch of roast meats, baked potatoes and kumara, followed by steamed pudding, lemon meringue pie and the ubiquitous tinned fruit salad, with great glass jugs of cream. She hadn't eaten a meal like this since she'd been with Ratapu's father. Extraordinarily good steamed pudding. Just like the one Roma's Mum used to make. Not her sort of food, not, she guessed, the sort of food most of the women here are used to. Was this a pointer for the future? Welcomes from the Tangata Whenua were now de rigeur — was catering by the local Maori group also to be part of the necessary ritual? She hoped not. She'd grown fond of the sort of food that shared women's lunches produced — big bowls of various and mysterious salads, french bread and cheese and manifold sprouts and fruit. I really must do a Maori language course next term. I can't stand the awful boredom of another welcome, not understanding a word. Well, not more than the odd word. One speaker had talked for twenty-five minutes this time. She always became excruciatingly aware of her bad back at such times. Next time Ratapu stopped over she'd ask him whether he still had the tapes left from the ATI course he'd done.

As the lunch ended the women involved in the organisation of the food and welcome and entertainment spoke. There were four in all, two of them extremely fat, and each was followed by songs.

"You've been good ladies — nice ladies — and if some of you were a bit scratchy last night with everything running so late — well we were too . . ."

That's nice she thought, having politely hidden her irritability. I'm glad some of us were obviously a bit scratchy.

"And it's good to see you old women here — so many white heads. It's good to learn from our elders — for them to be handing their knowledge on to you."

She thought of Jay's "too mature for me Mum", and wondered how old you had to be to be an elder.

Sitting on the steps outside, drinking Nescafe in the weak winter sun, she talked to a thin and elegant journalist who'd written an unpublished and unpublishable novel and wanted to tell her why it had gone wrong.

"The characters lacked continuity. You need a story — a story to cause interaction and show the characters in action. I just didn't have a story."

She listened, murmuring little noises of agreement or deprecation, but the comments worried her. Surely stories were passe. Hadn't Woolf back in 1930 in *The Waves* abolished stories for ever? Yet she knew she still read for the story. But what is a story?

"Josephine Brooks, aged 52, a heavily built woman with a distinctly aquiline nose and hooded eyes, untidy but colourful clothes, sat on the steps of her old school talking animatedly with . . . with . . ." (she looked at the journalist's lapel) "with Annabel Turvison, an elegant dark-haired fortyish journalist . . ."

But that wasn't a story for she and Annabel were about to get up and part and there would be no ongoing interaction, no continuity — no novel. Having said all there was to be said, they picked up their cups, and carried them back to the kitchen where the girls of the concert group were deep frying chunks of luncheon sausage in batter, and telling jokes in a circle around the very fat woman who had organised the food. They, the outsiders, were ignored as they stood apologetically cups in hand. Annabel went back to the famous novelist's workshop — she'd been attending it through all the sessions.

Josie, feeling full and sluggish and disillusioned thought of following Jay. But there was a writing workshop by a Wellington woman who actually taught creative writing. She ought to go to it. She was late, not able to find any directions as to which classroom it was in. The ten or so women there were faceless in a blur of embarrassment. They exchanged names for a second time (Oh God!) and then took slips of paper containing character traits and wrote about and role-played the characters. Josie enjoyed this sort of thing. She was good at it — all those years of teaching, if nothing else, had given her confidence and a loud voice in a group. She was paired off with Jay's friend — the fortyish skinny tatty woman Melinda (there was no surname on her name tag). They were a hypochondriac and an eternal optimist trapped together in a lift. They were both very good at it. She enjoyed her role and the way the other woman played up to and with her enormously. When they finally read out their pieces she'd liked them all, but particularly Mel's which was about an affair a woman had with the husband of a friend. It sounded awfully familiar. So she wasn't a lesbian after all.

After the session she stood on the balcony surrounding the hall with Mel while she smoked.

"Well, that redeemed the weekend for me!"

"Bloody good facilitating!" And they talked a bit, agreeing, on what made a good facilitator.

"Are you staying for the closing session?"

"Are you?"

This felt like the beginning of a story. She could feel the weight of future interactions stretching out ahead. "That moment of recognition" — recognition of what?

Melinda was grinning at her. Her face wrinkled around her eyes.

"Fuck, she's lovely," Josie thought in astonishment — "quite lovely." Then the moment vanished, leaving her looking at a pleasant, friendly, intelligent woman.

"Can I give you a lift somewhere? I'm a friend of Jay's. We're at Art School together. Both second year."

"Oh yes — I wondered — that is — no. I've got a car. But look, I live very close — in Grey Lynn. If you'd like to come we could have our own closing session — talk about the weekend and about writing?"

"I'd love to. Shall I just follow you? Are you in the carpark?"

This is the beginning Josie thought. The beginning of a poem, or a novel, or an affair.

She has to be a dyke, she thought.

Morgaine

Annabel Fagan

I was born in Muritai, Whanganui-a-Tara. The hills surrounding our house were wild and woolly with bush as far back as the eye could see. So I grew up wild and woolly, and I haven't changed.

From the room I was born in you could see out over Tara's great bay even to the South Island. I grew up with a visual wealth that stays with me wherever I go. My dreams are always there.

I skite too about Muritai. Yes, I say, that's where me and Katherine Mansfield grew up.

Laughing Girl

I'm a funny lesbian. Always the same, laughing and happy, good fun, they tell me. It's true, I am. I laugh and smile and talk all the time. But it's also a lie. Like the proverbial clown I cry with a smile. That way I always have friends.

I chuckle ripping open my skin with razor blades or popping little pills. How are you, they say. I'm fine, I laugh like frog, my throat on fire with iodine. Tincture. Doesn't kill I discovered, only tortures, tears up the flesh like drilling a road, tosses bits and pieces around, leaves a slash there, a deep pit here, with blood thick at the bottom. I suppose that blood put out the fire in the end — it wasn't me. I didn't do it. I am a fire sign and fought for the flames that roared and bellowed in my throat. Nevertheless I felt cheated. I thought I would die. You deceived me, I could have laughed to the chemist.

You're thick Mr Chemist, the young woman said, you lie by omission and pretend you are dead. You're a dick Master Chemist, the little girl said, I'll gouge out your eyes and eat them on bread.

I've tried telling the truth but no-one believes me. Everyone says, go on, and they have disbelief in their eyes. Go on. What a good joke their eyes say. The trouble is, I laugh telling the truth as well. Laugh and the world laughs with you. Fat lot of good that is.

When I sliced into the flesh of my arms it was as easy as cutting up raw liver — but the liver didn't heal over and scar. It was not alive. Instead the cat chewed it, her head moving from side to side with the effort. You must have lousy chewing teeth cat, the meat is not tough.

But I am. Tough and strong and laughing. That girl's tough, I heard them say on the strawberry patch, wouldn't like to tangle with her. How'd you get those scars, they ask, in a fight? Yeah, I answer, cool. (Not yeah, YES dear, insists my mother, but I don't listen. Ye-aaah.) And I stomp proudly along my row squeezing strawberries from their leaves like pimples from my chin, their mess smearing onto my fingers and behind my nails. In a fight, I say to my bare feet which pad along either side of me. They must mean with knives. I'm in awe of myself. Me! I say pleased. Me, who has never physically fought. Now I have laughter and toughness — the one for friends, the other for foes, eh. Let no-one tangle with me, and I swing jauntily along like the elephant I pretended to be when I was very small, bent over and vulnerable, my trunk before me. Ya poo, girl's play, shouts a big boy, fitting his bare, rugby-playing foot around my 4-year-old bottom and kicking me onto the concrete. Ha hoo, he yells, another Indian hits the dust. Years later, when that boy breaks his back in a scrum I chortle to myself, can't even kick your own balls around now, I say. But he recovers and lines up 1, 2, 3, 4, 5, 6 children. No permanent damage.

I liked being tough among the strawberries, especially when it rained and us dykes who drove out every morning from town, wore huge black plastic bags with holes torn for head and arms. Hard cases we looked, bare, rain-spattered limbs, muddy feet, and — best of all — they couldn't play the radio so there was peace under the open grey sky. Muddy and aching with rain seeping in, I felt excited and free. I didn't have to talk to anyone, I didn't have to laugh and yet I was surrounded by women. I loved those days of parting the wet, luxuriant bushes, swishing aside the shiny green leaves, while my fingers searched of their own accord for the centre, the warm fruit — an incentive for any lesbian. I picked them to fill my basket, but the plumpest I would put into my mouth, covering them with my lips and biting them gently, one at a time till the sweet juices filled my mouth and ran down my throat. A-a-h, strawberries like that are never found in shops. You non-berry picking, stay-at-home dykes sure missed out, my sisters.

Did any of the others feel that way? Did they touch the berries with such homage and lust, with such bursting, tender feelings as I did then but never have again, not once, not ever. They went, the strawberries, gradually plucked away, the riotous bushes up-rooted and withered dry. Who did it, did I?

Once, four of the city girls, as they called us — are the city girls here? they said every morning even though the patch was only half an hour out along the north western motorway — once, four of us had a mud fight. Not me. I'm not partial to wallowing in anything really, except of course, strawberries, and my own misgivings. But they rolled and played in folds between the long hummocks, covering themselves in so much swampy mud, sluggish like thick gravy, I could scarcely tell them apart. The others, the regular workers, nudged one another, jesus look at the city girls, they said, look! Down in the mud those four dykes were coiling and twining like earthworms, dancing their way through the slush, while I watched and wished I was there too, marshy and rank and touching. And the others, the hets, or so they said, although all women picking strawberries are lesbians to me — the hets sniggered in wonder and muttered as they readied to leave, gathering bags and shoes and full punnets of the thinner berries, sold to the workers cheap.

Who were those four?

We'd changed our names on the patch but I never got them right. I didn't change mine, I couldn't, it would have been like altering my face, putting on makeup and I'd have panicked that no-one would know me, lost behind an alien name like a mask. But the other four did and I was forever getting it wrong, calling Claire who was really Megan, Jean. And calling Jean who was really Pip, Claire. Or one of the workers would talk about Marian and I'd say, who? Oh I was confused. So I don't remember who was down there in the mud that day, that dyke-day on the patch. Only that they were there and I envied them. Finally they leapt up and ran, shouting and laughing, mud falling from them in dollops. Back at the shed I hosed those dirty ones down while they whimpered and lifted their feet, gasping and shifting like dogs having their bath. I was clean except for my feet which I washed as usual while the others stood about and dripped.

Were they impelled into such theatre by the heady smell of the strawberries and the powerful presence of all us women, earthy and sweating and fundamental under the morning sky?

I loved them and thought I was loved in return. I loved everyone during my intoxicating, joyful emergence into the lesbian world. The original born-again woman. I wasn't aware I was a laughing girl. I didn't know I'd missed something when I was eighteen months old or eight years — a vital step, and there are many vital steps so they say, and if you miss one, if one is denied you, you are crippled somewhere, in your limbs, or mind or in your heart. With me it was my heart and I didn't know it. I lifted it up to love but love couldn't get past the plaster and bandages I had wound there for protection. My barrier. That's right. I didn't know then that all my life I'd been laughing and laughing — with derision at myself.

After I left the patch I travelled a bit, reaching out, or so I thought. But only my arms stretched up. My body was turned away and my heart stuttered. Everyone could feel that. Everyone but me. I had plenty of friends — my laughter drew them, and my toughness maybe. But I was always outside a circle. Here, were parties and pubs and dinners, concerts and dances and softball, but there, there inside, was special and warm, a belonging place as mysterious to me as within a womb. Everyone entered, everyone found a soft opening place and they moved effortlessly through when they pleased — at least all the women I knew did. Except those who went mad. I didn't go mad, of course I didn't go mad. But I never found the acquiesing, viscous entrance, the elemental threshold which led everywhere. Instead I ran round and round outside, shouting and laughing, drawing attention to myself, attracting people who ran with me for a time and then disappeared — into There. Leaving me.

It happened and it happened. And after a while I noticed and felt . . . trollopish, used and abused, an employee. I shrank down and shook with disgust and anger at myself. I thought I wasn't a worthy person.

I took to holding my hand, tenderly, reassuringly as if I were my own special woman. Even in bed; particularly in bed. Sometimes I held it aggressively, possessively, butchdykishly, encircling myself, see! One woman broke through, some of the way. She pulled my hands apart and held them herself — but to me then, it felt bad, like the christmas with my sister a few years ago.

We went to a party. The men stood at one end and gabbled wisely, drinking great quantities of beer, while the women sat and talked. Someone who played "I Am Woman" and my sister and I said, let's get up, let's dance, let's do it together. We formed a circle, some reluctantly, some gleefully, some with fear — and took hands. We danced and sang not noticing the men becoming silent to us. Hey lemme join, yelled one. No, we said daringly, high on ourselves, no you can't, this song is only for us, for women. The track was three minutes long but seemed forever as we danced in our triumphal circle, kicking up our legs and roaring our song: I AM INVINCIBLE. But the men couldn't stand it. Like police they surrounded us and battened us into submission, back into wives, girlfriends, and sisters-in-law. Two men caught hold of a woman and me and wrenched us apart. Another united his two fists and smashed them down like a hammer on two clasped hands. Shocked and dismayed, we submitted. We were told off, taken home, blamed for spoiling the party.

Well, this time felt like that for some reason, but I had it all wrong as usual, so I spoiled the party, it was me. There was no physical violence — I knew that. I thought there was emotional violence and maybe there was in a way. Perhaps she was saying, let me in I want to love you, and I heard, let me in I want to hurt you. Maybe my laughing made me deaf or I could have been too afraid to listen. (Sukey, sukey, sukey, too scared, too scared, sukey, sukey BABY). In any case she had to force herself in — was that violence? Did she do too much while I was mute. I needed to do it, not her, but I didn't know that. Stupid. Yet a small love, as fragile as a crystal wine glass lay deep inside me, but I couldn't tell her, I simply pushed her away with my laughter and my chat — then hated her for the rejection, eh.

I imagined myself as open, instead I held so tight I could scarcely breathe. Only if I shouted and laughed would I not suffocate, but my breath came out in such great gasps it exhausted me. Surviving is not living. I wanted passion. Instead I sought attention in the bin — and got it. How I got it.

We were a ward full of women who were watched through a hole in the wall. The doors were heavily closed but the eye in the wall never even blinked. During the day it was pale blue, at night pale yellow, that eye. I watched and watched it watching me. I thought of it as being one large collective eye belonging to the staff — the nurses and psychiatrists, deadly in their office making plans. I thought of them as a cyclops, passing the eye from one to the other and putting it to the hole, while they, blind and powerful, continued with their intentions.

Yes Doctor.

No.

Blue Pills.

Red Pills.

The Needle.

E.C.T.

Whispers went round our ward: that woman is an insomniac — never sleeps. And she's a nymphomaniac, imagine! And her, look at her all dark and thin, she was a ward sister who went mad herself. Felicity there, she's suicidal. She had a friend, a male friend who used to visit her and her husband. One day she came home and found them in bed together, the husband and him. She tried to cope but it went on and on, week after week. They talked to each other in Latin in front of her, she said, made jokes and laughed. She joined them in bed a few times but when that didn't work she despaired, took pills and landed up here. Deeply disturbed, they say. I'm not surprised. And old Mrs Tasman, not so old as she looks, she's dying of a brain tumour so they stuck her in. That woman, always in her nightie and losing things — too many ECTs, that's why, makes her dribble. She's here for depression. She lost her ring once and asked me to find it, said she'd lost it down her front, poor thing. I put my hand down, past her breasts and stomach, right down to her pubes, her skin was cold and wet, sweaty from the shocks eh. I didn't find it, she was really upset. She cried. My wedding ring, she said. She was all loose and fleshy, she's had eight kids. Probably into the change.

I looked at the women, all those women, vivid, even here. They weren't mad and I wasn't mad, are any of us ever mad? What were we doing here? What was I doing here, a sane person, in a place where a certain form of madness was assigned to us and we received it like a gift. (The word gift in German means poison.) OUT, OUT, quickly. Out from under the eye. I told the doctor, it was a mistake to come, I said and after all, I'd entered of my own accord and could surely leave the same way. But, Hah, they said and captured me, injecting me painfully and deliberately into a buttock muscle. WHAT! they said, you can't just go when you like, how dare you, we know what's best, not you. Only we know when you are ready to face Out There, the Infinitely Superior World.

So I tried to escape. One evening I fled down the big main staircase and out into the formal garden — flat lawns, flowerbeds and shrubs. But they were quick and cunning. They surrounded the area and left only one way open — the path, doors, and stairs back into the ward. And while I crouched under a bush in my nightdress, hunted and afraid, they moved close, their torchlights round and yellow in the dark, whispering amongst themselves, beating towards me, inexorably advancing, until I was flushed out, a terrified animal. I ran straight back into their trap as they knew I would and they followed and bagged me up in a strait-jacket where I shivered and screamed and hated them.

Not long after, they did let me go. I was too much for them, ha, ha. They wanted a ward full of passive zombies and I never stayed drugged enough. But they threw me out when I least expected and that disturbed me. I'd given up a little, wasn't ready and I've always preferred to be ready, to choose the time myself. I liked to mull over future events, pore over maps and timetables and be satisfied I'd done every bit of my homework. So for a while I was stunned out there. Where was my routine, my breakfast at seven, my bath at eight, my security? One thing I learned: never again would I voluntarily put myself in a place where they tried to smother my mind, where I had no choice in anything. Never again I vowed. Why, they wouldn't even let me kill myself in there, the pigs. And they should have, because it was their fault, their idea, not mine.

The psychiatrist said, have you ever wanted to commit suicide? I answered, no, I'm a lesbian. And he said, don't be silly, so I never mentioned it again, but I did try to kill myself.

Out there, in the hostel they'd chosen for me, I tried and tried to wash the bin out of me. I knelt under water and rubbed and washed repeatedly. I didn't laugh but cried this time, knowing that salt could cleanse. I hated the other women, their skins were grimy and grey, did they ever clean themselves? I was certain they never touched their grey necks and grey heels. They made me sick. I was grimy too, the world was. I again tried suicide — this was the iodine attempt which I told no-one about, but stayed in bed all day after my room-mates had gone to work, breathing fire and crying, crying still instead of laughing. That was the turning point, the tears which finally cleansed and soothed me, the incessant weeping no-one noticed — maybe they were too scared, the poor nutty one, she might become dangerously deranged and set us on fire too. Of course they did ask, someone asked, I remember, and I laughed a little answering.

But mostly I lay while my body worked things out, talked softly to itself and I was quiescent, a nothing — I didn't listen, didn't interfere. That was good because it did all right, it did well. When finally I got up and went outside, I saw brightness and colour again, I could smell smells, see the air swirling, catch it in my hands like dusty silver and breathe it in and out quietly, like other people. I could clasp trees to me in friendship and speak to flowers. I was glad of dicky chemists.

And I remembered a time on the patch all those months ago when a woman's voice, two rows away, was heard saying, Maudie's gay you know. And I stood up and shouted, so am I, I'm gay. And Nikki next to me instantly straightened and said, I am too, I'm a lesbian. And shouts from the other three came to us as they stood — me too, I'm a lesbian. I am. I am. I am. And the whole patch stopped work and unfolded like a pack of cards righting itself. All the women stood tall as if to say, we might be, some of us are. I smiled now, seeing the boss, a young man, walking amongst us puzzled, this had not happened before, not in our season. What's the matter, he called, why have you all stopped, what's gone wrong? Nothing's wrong, I answered, nothing at all.

Leaning against my friend the tree, feeling its chunky, reassuring bark, I knew it must again be the season, the sweet strawberry season. Ahhhh, I sighed, a kind of peaceful realisation spreading from me to the tree and back again. I will leave this block of rooms as I left the other. I will find myself a little place and take in a cat flat-mate. And then, I'll go again and pick strawberries . . .

Annabel Fagan
The Woman Who Talks to Trees

No-one knows her surname. When new people come into the area, the kind who bother with old people, they approach Barbara on the street, breaking into her reverie. "Gidday", he says, holding out his hand, "I'm Pete Simpson from across the road, this is my wife Pat. Pete and Pat eh, easy to remember." Barbara says, "I'm Barbara." She touches his plump rough hand with her soft, thin one. Skin not her own. I don't remember names. I'll have forgotten yours before you reach the gate. But I might think of peas. She looks at them and smiles at herself and they smile back. She likes her name: rough, wild, uncultured, a foreigner, a barbarian. Barbara. I am all of those, a person apart, differently cultured. Yes I am certainly a wild and rough and revelling foreigner. But not in the dictionary sense, not in that way. It's me in the dictionary because I say so, not because they say so. My definition of their definition, she thinks with satisfaction, my words. I'm lucky, I have a choice.

The neighbours say, there she goes, Mrs Whatshername. They don't like to say Barbara. They feel awkward, like grown up children. Look at her muttering away, poor old dear, though not so old, late sixties I'd say and she's spry enough. Walks and walks with that dog of hers, every day, rain or shine, down to the beach, up to the shops. Keeps herself fit. Tough old bird and she dresses tough eh, jeans and shirts and running shoes. If you didn't know, you'd swear she was a man. Especially with that hair-cut.

Oh I'm far from being a man, says Barbara. There are times I feel so swollen with my womanliness that I am doubled, tripled in it. As if I need three of me to contain it, all this plenitude which seems about to spill over, burst out of my one spare body to form another and another, all dressed as I dress, in jeans and shirt and running shoes. Oh, I'm a woman all right. A three-fold woman. And if you don't approve of my jeans, what would you think of my socks. They're very bright, I love my socks. I have a shocking pink pair and a lime green and several with black and blue and red stripes, my favourites, nothing like them in my young days. I have yellow for summer and black ones too, very smart. Not white. White has no colour and after a while the socks look dead. In town they think I'm buying for my grandchildren, but they're for the trees. I dress up for the trees. I pull up my jeans and say, look, see what colour I'm wearing today. And the trees always answer. If it's a festive season they sway and dance and creak and show pleasure that way. My feet in their colours appear to dance back even though I myself don't dance much any more. At other times they just want a hug. I put my arms around one and stay there for an infinity of time simply embracing. Later I am stiff but not cold and when I put my fingers to my cheek I find a pattern which has faded away by the time I am home and look in the mirror. But I'm sure it was beautiful, her sign to me like a song on my skin. Which I'll never see, I don't have to, I know what the words say. I know they're magic and wise words because I'm a magical and wise woman. And I never did look my age. I'm seventy-seven. A spell-binding age. And as for muttering, I'm talking, talking to the trees. I am a woman who talks to trees.

Barbara walks along her street with Dawson her big, bitsa, black and tan dog. Bit of alsation there, say the neighbours. And collie. Could be a bit of doberman too or maybe huntaway. Nice-looking dog.

Beautiful, says Barbara. You are beautiful aren't you Dawson. The dog so addressed, sits immediately, his tail swishing the ground. Yes, yes, I am if you say so, say it again, he implores. You are so beautiful, Barbara obliges and Dawson grins and skips away, ecstatic.

That old lady, comments a neighbour, one of the kids heard her the other day, saying sorry to a tree. Donny thought she was talking to him and stopped, but no, she actually addressed a tree and put her hand on it like you do when you're telling Mary something. They go a bit . . . You Know, at that age, eh. Poor, old thing, probably lonely, I'll see if she needs anything done. Mostly they're better off in a home like your mum, but I must say she seems to do for herself all right. At least she only keeps one cat, not like the other old biddies around, feeding all the strays. They're like pied pipers with all those cats.

I'm not lonely. I have the trees. And wouldn't you apologise if you banged into someone, says Barbara. And don't you ask for things instead of just taking. Well I ask for lemons and tamarillos. I ask for feijoas and they fall softly into my hands. They never refuse me my friends, never.

And I talk to my animals. Miaow, miaow, miaow, I say to my cat, which isn't enough so I poke her to get her attention. I love touching her on the thickest part of her fur and watching half my finger disappear. I poke her gently and she lazily looks up. Waddayuwant, she says. If she's sleeping on her chair and I'm reading on mine but suddenly feel like a chat, I call her name, Carlotta, Carlotta, Carlotta, I murmur winningly. And although her ears shoot in my direction, the rest of her doesn't move. CARlottah, CARlottah, CARlottah, I call more urgently, but only her ears live, probing the air like antennae — will it be worth it? I become frantic, look at me Carlotta, I shout. I bang things, stamp my feet but refuse to get up, it has become a contest. I'll stand on my head for you, I scream, if I could. She uncurls slightly, yawns, goes back to sleep. No dice. It's only after I've desperately smashed up my unread newspaper that she finally looks at me. Yeah. Quick, now I really have to work. Her own voice has matured with age. She miaows hoarsely, her chirrups and purrs have deepened but she prefers me high-toned which is exhausting. She also likes her name said over and over with some variation in pitch and pronunciation but the assonance unchanged. Cats are very particular. Carlottie - Pottie - Wottie, I squawk like an idiot. Ooooooooh, dear little Lottie, Snottie, Tottie, knowing I'd die if anyone heard. Carlottie, my sweet hottie-bottie, I twitter, while she, if I'm lucky, if I've caught her at the right time, that as well, when there isn't a fly on the wall or a bird on the roof, then she sits up and simpers at me, flutters her lashes, and if her fur weren't so lush, I'd see dimples appear on her fat cheeks as she smiles and smiles and smiles like the queen.

Dawson is always with Barbara, on the beach, on any of her walks, to the shops, through parks, around the area. If he's intrusive during her celebration with a tree, she takes him away a little bit, tells him to sit, to lie down, to stay, good boy. And he does. He's interested in her friendship with trees. He watches and listens. Well, he likes trees too in his own way. They have their own unbiased relationship. With Dawson I converse in my natural tone of voice. I like talking to him because his ears go up and down in a highly intelligent way which shows he's listening — the equivalent of a person nodding I suppose. He looks at me and takes everything in, except when he's embarrassed, which he often is, when I get too soppy or swear. Carlotta laps up soppiness and couldn't care less if I swore. Cats are never embarrassed. But dogs are. At such times Dawson turns his eyes up to the ceiling or stares fixedly to one side. I can not listen, he says. In deference to his sensibilities I often modify my language and tend to stick to subjects like the weather and what we'll have for dinner. He likes that. Dawson is a very basic sort of being, what is what, is what with Dawson, like talking to a three-year-old child.

But on the beach at sunset the rich, brown parts of his fur become burnished by the sun. They light up, his whole brown face with its black-rimmed eyes, takes on a glow that so overwhelms Barbara, she asks him to sit so she can just look, oh Dawson. He sits and gazes nobly and patiently out over the sea while she looks and looks at the flooding sun and him, reflecting each other in their sheen as if they're momentarily related.

When Barbara was a little girl, a little, skinny girl — then I was skinny, now I'm thin, there's a difference, says Barbara — she and her friends used to play house on a rise under a small forest of pine. Their house was a very exciting place, having several storeys going up the wee hill with many rooms connected to one another by steps and paths. It was exciting and dangerous to the small Barbara, walking along the narrow paths, climbing up the hard steps from the bedrooms to the kitchen, the kitchen to the lounge. That's why she loved that house. It had been dug out of the earth a hundred years ago, decided Barbara, this huge house running up and down and everywhere inside it. The ground in the rooms was bouncy and orange with pine-needles. She loved snuggling down on them with her very best friend to sleep at night, closing her eyes and smelling the pines and waking up three minutes later when it was morning. The rooms were only big enough for two, comfortable hollows with roots sticking out of the ceilings. Nothing grew under the pines except the children and, in spring, daffodils, jonquils, snowdrops, which jumped up when no-one was looking and were suddenly there, elegant and sweet-smelling. Haven't we got a pretty house and garden, they said.

Barbara loved the piney smell of the trees. She'd climb up and up, even though she was frightened, but not right to the top, never to the top, not even half-way. No, she'd find a safe, sitting place a little way up and stay there for ages, sniffing the smells all around, her hands sticky with resin, her bare legs scratchy against the bark. "Where are you, where are you, where are you", sings out her best friend. "I'm up here in heaven", Barbara sings back.

Once in a while Barbara catches a bus to town and gets off at the park where she has many special friends. She visits the Moreton Bay Figs which remind her of great elephants with their grey, smooth, skins and many hanging trunks and tails. She is drawn to them, would like to caress them, lie skin to skin, but they intimidate her and she touches them with respect not affection.

There are young Kauri too and as she passes, Barbara shouts to them encouragingly. Lovely day, she calls. You look well, very healthy. You'll be massive in no time. In a hundred years, she thinks but doesn't say. Sometimes she pats them. Good girls.

One tree, quite young, but not so young as the Kauri, dances for all she is worth, her branches flung akimbo. She is dancing without movement but quite passionately this still day in the park. I can see you're enjoying yourself, says Barbara, I remember the feeling. A piece of bark hangs loose on her trunk as if it's come untucked from somewhere and Barbara reaches in and touches the slippery white wood. Like lifting a Tee-shirt and tickling a tummy. Do excuse me she says, I couldn't resist it.

A very large tree stands at the main entrance. She has a tall trunk with short, leafy branches right at the top — like the curls I put on all my drawings of girls when I was little. The tree wears a modest skirt of creeper, pale green and yellow which encircles her body neatly and tidily up to her waist. At the bottom it billows out over the earth and looks very pretty and clean. In winter the skirt is flecked with brown from falling leaves, giving it a proper, tweedy, warm sort of look. I like your skirt, Barbara always says politely. She finds the tree very feminine but doesn't regard this as demeaning, which once she might have. To each her own, thinks Barbara, and she might be in fancy dress for all I know, getting ready for the ball.

Across from the clothed tree is another, Barbara's favourite and a total contrast. You sit with your strong thighs thrust upwards, no frills on you. Instead you wear your pubic hair, bright green and riotous which I do admire and long to stroke. It is sheeny and damp and spreads where it will, this enticing moss of yours which beckons, put your lips to mine. You flaunt it for all to see who would see and I see. I see and see. I acknowledge you from my own source, my hills and valleys and mountains, whose foliage wispy now, was once exuberant like yours. You are brazen and unrestrained, a fest of a tree, says Barbara.

At home she tells Carlotta and Carlotta doesn't turn away and wash. She listens, her yellow eyes slanting, her ears still. And as she hears, her fur loosens and fans out, its colour changing from grey to silver as if steeped in the light of her own personal moon. She crouches, full and round, an enormous little cat.

I remember long ago when I was young, going out of our holiday house, says Barbara. It was late afternoon, the tide was almost high, the Pohutukawa were waving to the sea and me. Come, they said. I climbed into the comfortable lap of one and sat, leaning back against a wide branch. I was unhappy, lonely, for what reason I don't know, I can't remember, only that I often felt that way. I cried and the sea wept back as it surged below in sympathetic melancholy. I cried and then stopped. It was getting dark. I sat, and then . . . I disappeared. I disappeared into an arras of evening mist, into soft sounds which touched and reached, and felt like the sea on my skin. I disappeared into the very core of the tree, into a mystical, sensual place, which my head doesn't remember but the rest of me does, oh yes. I was gone for hours, four or five, they said, we called and called, where were you? I don't know, I answered.

Carlotta stretches, settles, becomes an ordinary grey cat. But before she sleeps, she looks once more at Barbara. I know, she says.

Fran Marno

Linley Dearson

I live in a supportive, central Auckland household where the teapot is always warm and the dishes are never done.

I love summer living, days at the beach, good friends, food and laughter.

I believe ageism is as insidious as racism and sexism, and have dreams of a tolerant and accepting society where no-one is made to feel alone or outcast.

The Power and the Glory
Daisy and Lilly — two 80 year old lesbians

It was just lately that Daisy had really begun to bug Lilly. She could put up with her snoring at night — although her blocked sinuses had made it a feat of endurance. She could even put up with her new trendy car (a Mitsubishi) — and the way she revved it in the morning. She'd suffered her revving for the last 40 years so she wasn't going to start complaining about it now. She was after all a tolerant woman and at 80 she wasn't going to change Daisy's delightful idiosyncrasies.

No, the thing that really bugged her was the new-found group — a Women's Ritual group that Daisy had attached herself to, although Lilly often wondered whether the group had attached itself to Daisy.

Every Tuesday evening at 7.00, Daisy revved out of the yard — a simple, conventional elderly lesbian woman. Every Tuesday evening at 11.00, sometimes 12.00, Daisy revved back, waking the neighbours, shrieking about Hecate and Demeter and Goddess knows who else. She had an added glittery and slightly wild look about her. It was this change that niggled Lilly. It usually lasted all day Wednesday, Thursday and after a particularly potent Tuesday night sometimes into Friday.

The house just wasn't the same any more. Little stories started appearing in the most bizarre places, one in the toilet, Daisy said to relieve constipation. She also took to long and very ill-timed conversations with her dream figures. Coronation St was dispensed with to engage in such outlandish activities.

It was definitely time for Lilly to confront Daisy, or she could see the possibility of a separation very much on the horizon.

On a wild and stormy September night Lilly decided to present the facts.

"My dearest," she murmured, while Daisy sat in a Lotus position on the hearth (not a good start. Daisy did not like being disturbed while she was trying

48

to look "disciplined"). "My dearest I'm worried about you. I wonder could you be showing your age a little attending that Ritual group. It just doesn't seem to do you much good!" Lilly prided herself on her directness.

Daisy shut the left nostril and continued to take a long — very long — breath in through her right nostril. An ominous sign from a Taurean woman. Lilly continued. "The neighbours have twice complained about the revving of the car, especially at 12.00 at night. An 'ungodly' hour for anyone." The last pun was well rehearsed and she tittered slightly.

Daisy remained Buddha-like, although her breath was louder and more pronounced. Things were definitely hotting up.

Lilly knew all the signs — the post, post menopausal flush, the heavy breathing, the rigid nostril-work and, above all, that "holier than thou" expression that Daisy had perfected. It was one of the variety that would make even the Virgin Mary confess to indecencies . . .

Lilly could feel her backbone straighten. One had to remain intractable when meeting an immovable force. She paused, then remembering the "I" statements, plunged onwards.

"I am feeling quite frankly bored by all this egotistical, self-indulgent hocus-pocus. What has happened to Animal Rights? What has happened to our Active Lesbian Oldies group? our political campaigning?"

Bang! Daisy had slammed the door behind her. The storm that night knocked three plants over and one stone from the top of the toilet shelves.

Inside nothing raged.

"Night Daisy," muttered Lilly.

"Night," muttered Daisy.

Bed socks and nighties were firmly in place. The electric blanket was warm, backs were resolutely turned on each other. Not a single hair touched — two bodies like stranded whales lay beached on each side of the bed — stony still. Both were "asleep" in record time. No snoring. No moving. Not a sound.

"It is going to be a long night," Lilly mused.

It was around 4 am when the stone blown off the shelf clattered to the floor.

"Wretched, ruddy stones," Lilly moaned. And it was at this time when circumnavigating the evening's proceedings for the ninetieth time, she hit upon her idea. An idea that swept in suddenly, engulfing Lilly in a wave of bubbling excitement. At last, exulted, she fell into a deep sleep.

Tuesday came with its usual regularity and Daisy (the simple, conventional and very well-prepared lesbian that she was) revved out of the back yard. She was dressed in a flowing, white gown. A garland of daisies wrestled with her hair. She had spent the last three days immersed in literature on Persephone and the very act of closing the back door had taken on shades of emerging from the Underworld. The ritual was all she had dreamed of. There, bathed in the light and warmth of kindred spirits she had scrubbed herself clean of the week's turmoil. She had wantonly frolicked and delicately rejoiced.

At 12.05 she flew home. The flight was, as always, haphazard, with Daisy singing to full-lung capacity. She smiled benevolently at the waving and tooting traffic officers en route. A happy bunch of men.

Even before reaching the house she had woven the delights of the evening into the ecstacy of seeing Lilly's reproachful face. Like a cold shower after a languid rest in the sun, both were indispensable to the other.

"Lilly," she sparkled, opening the front door and floating into the bedroom. "Lilly . . ."

The bed lay undisturbed. No jug was boiling in the kitchen. There was no flushing of the toilet.

"Yoo-ho Lilly," Daisy called, "I'm home."

Silence.

Daisy sat numb-founded. Never had Lilly done this to her before — never! Visions of Lilly covorting passionately with Sybil (73, a librarian, politically correct and TERRIFYINGLY boring) festered in her brain.

"Go to it," she hissed savagely, "go to it. But don't you come running back to me Lilly Fergusson when the appeal of a younger woman wears a little bit thin — because, believe you me Lilly, I won't be here. I won't . . ." Daisy burst into loud and uncontrollable sobs, and Persephone sensing the return of Winter beat a hasty retreat.

"Anyone home?" a loud male voice boomed up the hall.

Daisy wiped her eyes, straightened her robe and pushed some daisies that had fallen onto the floor, back into her hair.

"Coming."

Two policemen stood shouldering Lilly on either side of the doorway. Lilly had that bedazzled look she gained when she had one too many sherries, or when love-making had been particularly sonorous.

Daisy had the scenario already mapped out. One glance was enough to provide her with all the information she needed. It was obvious.

Lilly had spent the evening frantically necking and drinking with Sybil. Coming home her head had been in such a daze she hadn't remembered which road to take . . .

"Daisy Wilcott," the moustached policeman began, "do you know this 'ere Lilly Fergusson. Your . . . mother? er, sister?"

"Lover" Daisy enunciated clearly, with a piercing glare at Lilly.

Both policemen blanched visibly. It had not been a routine night.

The policeman struggled on. "Er yes . . . well er . . . we suggest you keep Miss . . . er Lilly, at home for a few days. She was picked up a little non compos mentis . . . if you know what I mean. She was standing on the roof of her car spray-painting the wall of the City Council office. Something about" — the policeman consulted his notebook "OLD LESBIANS NEVER DIE, THEY JUST BECOME LESS VISIBLE."

Lilly's eyes met Daisy's. The thunder clapped.

"Oh Lilly," enthused Daisy, her passion mounting from the very basest of her Chakras . . . "Wherever did you get that from? It's so clever."

Both of them at this point couldn't remember how or when the policemen left, they had seemed to somehow dissolve into the dark of the night.

"Lilly," whispered Daisy many hours later, "do you think this little blot on your record will curb your style?"

"Not in the least," Lilly answered with conviction, "I've already thought of *another* slogan for next week. I tell you Daisy the power of the spray can is something to behold."

HILDA AND EDITH

Fran Marno

Angela

I am a Tai Tokerau woman living in Tamaki Makaurau. The short story I have written is the result of having lived by the Maunga in Tongariro National Park.

Maunga

I watched her as she clasped her hands behind her back. We smiled at each other. Well, here we were. The view was magnificent. Our home for a while. It ended up being much longer than a while but we couldn't complain. We were safe — reasonably. After all it was only a volcano that grew outside the large glass windows. Windows that reminded me of a movie screen. Very impressive. My sister clasped her hands tighter.

— A volcano?

— Yes, my Mother replied, oblivious of the terror she had inadvertantly engendered. I liked the idea of a volcano.

— It doesn't worry you does it?

I shifted my feet. It didn't worry me. I was convinced we were safe but my sister wasn't.

I looked at my reflection in the glass.

It was a long time since lava had poured down its sides, washing out bridges. Now it was assumed to be harmless.

I liked watching the smoke and had worked out a strategy if the worst should happen. Because we were so close to the volcano I had an advantage. I would know beforehand if it was to erupt. I would see the signs — very beautiful and dangerous. I wouldn't be afraid. I would calmly get dressed and wake the family. We would all escape. Ngauruhoe wouldn't get the best of me.

I used to sit at the window watching for change. More smoke, less smoke, more this, more that. When the mist came and covered the mountains I was sad, almost worried. It was a time for vigilance. What if it should erupt behind cloud? But it wouldn't do that. There had to be a warning sign. Nothing erupted without warning. I knew my facts.

Anyway, the mountains never looked real. They looked so perfect and because of that I was fooled into thinking that the mountains were close. Their closeness made them seem small. Too small for people, too small for the patupaiarehe.

I used to sit by those long sparkling windows gazing through my binoculars at the mountains — Tongariro, Ngauruhoe and Ruapehu. Each day I would look for something different, although I was never sure what. And who would believe a young girl sitting behind a glass wall? Still I watched closely.

When I first went into the mountains I found it hard to understand how they concealed so much. The slopes weren't smooth and flat but had hollows, peaks, crevasses, trees, people, even shops. They had looked so smooth and flat from behind the glass.

I spent hours watching. At night I would go for a walk — leave the window and go to the road. It was a wide cold road — straight. I didn't like to walk across it, so I would stand as close as I dared, watching for car lights. Jumping up and down, trying to keep warm, I would take the binoculars and gaze into the mountains. It was exciting to have more than one vantage point. Down here I seemed closer and somehow smaller, insignificant, or more so than when I was behind the glass. Even though I had mittens on I would slap my hands together to stop them going numb. I was afraid I might drop my binoculars or my hands might become frozen to them. I wouldn't sit down by the edge of the road but would stand on tip toes willing myself to grow while gazing cautiously through the binoculars. My mother said that they might as well be my third eye. I was careful not to be seen. Sometimes there would be one light on Ruapehu, sometimes ten or more. I stopped counting after ten. But I never saw a light on Ngauruhoe. If I was feeling especially brave I would take a torch and scan the bush for movement. Sometimes I felt it but never saw it.

I had a secret desire to walk straight across the flat bush clad land to the foot of the mountains — the exact spot where the land ended and the mountains began. I could see the spot from the road but I knew that as soon as I got close I would get confused, everything would merge together. There would be no clean cut line.

The days and months passed uneventfully sitting behind the glass window and watching, looking for a sign.

After a new fall of snow had covered the land I looked towards the mountains, now outlined sharply against the sky. I looked again. Mist was unravelling over and around Ngauruhoe, covering the mountain. I sat by the window for hours until my mother called me for dinner.

The next morning I woke early and went to the window. There was a layer of ash adorning Ruapehu — bright in contrast to the snow. Tongariro stood silently by. My gaze turned to Ngauruhoe but passed through emptiness to the plains beyond. The mountain had gone. All that was left was a large gap — an expanse of waste land, a hollow where its soft body of earth had once lain curled. I blinked in the harsh light. It couldn't be a trick of the glass. But who will believe me when I tell them that the mountain has moved?

Fran Marno

Miriam Saphira

I was born during the second world war at Kaimiro near Inglewood. My first love was the girl next door. I left school to work on the farm and left the farm to follow my girlfriend to teacher's college. On her rejection I got drunk, got pregnant and got married. Five children later I came out and am currently Secretary General of the International Lesbian and Gay Association.

Mrs Baker Said

Of course everybody makes mistakes and it is foolhardy not to admit to them from time to time. The difficulty seems to be that first impressions last longer than are truthfully useful and we can get tied up with much erroneous information if we are not more careful about what we may think we see. You can tell Mrs Baker that notion and she will agree with you but she never seems to be able to put it into practice.

Mrs Baker works at the tearooms with Mrs Wilson. It is a family business that the Wilsons established shortly after the new bakery was built in 1891. Ninety-four years later the building has much the same smells of freshly baked bread and cakes that can still be smelt down the main street of Inglewood.

Everybody knew the Wilsons tearooms. Even today everybody thought they knew everything about everybody here in Inglewood and if you were short of any information you could surely get it at the Wilsons tearooms. Tea was a homely affair like an old fashioned parlour. You had to walk through the brick and white tiled shop with its racks of crusty bread and cream filled cakes to reach the wooden tables covered in white starched lace cloths. The tables were placed close enough for a number of conversations to be picked up, especially if you sat at the more central ones.

On the sideboard there were rows of silver tea pots with tiered cake plates on sparkling, silver stems. The new white doilies showed the array of little cakes off to their best advantage: cork cakes dusted with icing sugar, their little tops almost popping with spiced flavour from yesterday's crumbed ginger gems. Of course in the old days icing sugar was all sugar and was much sweeter to put on the tip of your tongue. It still looks just as good though and it's sprinkled on the butterfly cakes and apple turnovers. How the raspberry squares and cherry cakes glisten with their pink and brown icing. The children all love to gaze at these dainty morsels, unable to make a choice, fearing that one might be just slightly more delicious, or larger than another.

There were windows on one side of the rooms looking towards the picture theatre but the customers could not see out once they had sat down as the lower halves of the windows were glazed with a bubbly glass.

If anything of any significance was happening Mrs Baker and Mrs Wilson were able to keep all the customers informed with good descriptions.

Today it was quiet. It was mid-week and there was no stock sale this week as they were only held once a month now. Mrs O'Byrne and her daughter Teresa were the only customers. They were waiting for the chemist across the road to make up the prescription for Teresa after their visit to the doctor. Teresa had had the day off school to enable her to get an appointment to see about her nose problems. As Mrs O'Byrne explained to Mrs Baker.

"I thought she would just grow out of her runny noses but it seems to be getting worse. Of course feeding out the hay doesn't help. Dr Watson seemed to think she has an allergy as well, to some of the grasses rather than to the animals. Of course you won't use that as an excuse to avoid weeding the garden will you, Teresa?"

"No, Mum." Teresa looks embarrassed at all this attention being paid to her.

"Allergies", said Mrs Baker, "can be very dangerous if you don't watch out for them. Mrs Hintz reacted to some medicine once and they had to rush her to the hospital. Very nearly lost her what with her breathing all stopped and that. She was in hospital for a week and there was poor Jim trying to run the farm and look after the little ones. It's too much for a young man to cope with. Of course Mrs Smith would have helped but she doesn't get on with her son-in-law and his mother is much too frail to manage young children now."

"It is a pity that she is missing school. Teresa's doing very well you know. She came top in biology and second in maths. And Jacob is doing well too and will be going to college next year."

"You are so lucky to have such hard working children, Mrs O'Byrne. So many of the children around here are skipping school and getting into trouble. Only yesterday Mr Scott was saying how young Clyde Jones' son was found in a dress and high heeled shoes at the station. Seems he was catching a bus to Wanganui to some club. I don't know what will happen to him. He was such a good swimmer too. He did so well at the National Championships and no one has beaten his butterfly record."

"Perhaps Father O'Reilly was meaning Timothy Jones when he was talking about the need for our sons to be sons and our daughters to be daughters. I couldn't understand what he was actually getting at."

"Oh, that'll be the shop." And Mrs Baker rushed out to the ringing of the bell.

Mrs O'Byrne turned to Teresa. "Hurry up with your cake Teresa instead of picking at it. We can't keep your father waiting and I want to get some more wool for Jacob's jersey."

Teresa was just about to pop the whole cake into her mouth when she suddenly stopped to watch the new customers walk into the tearoom. It was Timothy's cousin, Marie Robinson. This was bound to set both Mrs Baker and her mother off as Marie Robinson, swimming and running champion or not, was not liked by the adults of Inglewood.

"She's got a nerve coming in here," hissed Mrs O'Byrne. "I wonder who the young man is that she has got with her."

At that very moment Mrs Baker was saying to Mrs Wilson while she packed up the big order of savouries for the Lions meeting tonight at Ratapiko.

"That girl's got a nerve showing her face around these streets."

"She's with a young man. He doesn't look like he's from the Athletic Club. I'm sure I would recognise him," commented Mrs Wilson. She did not dislike Marie Robinson. In fact she always thought that if people had not been so antagonistic then Ann Green would probably still be living with her parents.

"It's not so strange that she's with a young man. None of the girls around here would want to be seen with her. Ann Green was such a nice girl too. Then that little minx started playing up to her and now she's gone right off the rails. Mrs Jeffries was saying that when she was seeing her sister in Wellington she was sure that she saw Ann Green. Her hair was cut off even shorter than those latest styles that the young women are wearing. All that lovely long blonde hair. I think that's awful, don't you, it's so unfeminine.

"And she was wearing a leather jacket like a bikie, and leaning all over this older woman. Mrs Jefferies was sure the older one was a lesbian not that I'm sure that Mrs Jefferies knows how to tell a . . ."

The bell from the tea room gave its distinctive little jangle. Mrs Wilson placed the lid on the last box of savouries and interrupted Mrs Baker.

"I'll go and serve them if you like," knowing that Mrs Baker would be unable to stop her curiosity and want to have a good look at the young man.

Mrs Baker was already threading through the archway to the tearoom.

"It's all right I'll get it."

Mrs Wilson looked after her and could not help but notice the strained look about Marie Robinson. It had not been easy for the young woman losing her father in a farm accident and being left to look after her crippled mother. She felt certain that Marie would not have stayed in Inglewood if her mother had not wanted to remain on their farmlet. Although her mother could cook and feed the hens it was up to Marie to milk the cow and grow the cut flowers they sold to the Stratford florists.

I wonder what is wrong with Marie. Surely Ann Green going away is not still upsetting her. Maybe they are both lesbians. Aren't they a bit obsessive like on that film, what was it called, "Sister George" or something like that?

Mrs Baker came bustling back into the shop.

"The young man is from Wanganui. He's inviting her down to some social. I bet she goes racing off and leaves her poor mother on her own. She has absolutely no regard for her mother, that little minx."

"I wonder what sort of social it is," Mrs Wilson's curiosity was also getting aroused.

"I think he said a lamb social. Maybe one of those Young Farmers' Club dos. Whatever it is, she'll be up to no good. She was suggesting that she bring Miss Sinclair, that young teacher at Tariki who is filling in for Mr Blanchard — I heard he will be out of the Base this Wednesday, and the operation was very successful — you don't think she has got designs on her do you? I thought Miss Sinclair was a nice young girl. I saw her riding one of the Fenwicks' horses and she looked such a pretty picture."

"But Roger Fenwick is getting engaged to Raewyn next weekend so she's too late if she thought she could catch him. These girls from the city are all the same, thinking it's romantic to marry a farmer. They have no idea how much hard work there is in running a farm and there's no money in it these days." Mrs Wilson stopped wiping the counter and began to straighten the tray of cakes.

"Good afternoon Mrs King. What can we do for you today?" Mrs Baker greeted a large ruddy faced woman carrying two large shopping bags.

"Well since you can't change the weather I guess I'll have a large white and half a dozen cup cakes. I've Rhonda coming over with the children for the evening while Tom is at the meeting."

"There should be a good crowd there tonight but these meetings don't seem to solve everybody's money worries do they?"

"The government has got to start listening to the farmers or we will all be down the drain and then where will the country be?"

Mrs King stared into the tea room and exclaimed.

"Goodness, is that young Marie Robinson sitting with a man! I thought she hated men."

"Yes," chipped in Mrs Baker. "It seems he is asking her to a Young Farmers' Club Dance at Wanganui. Maybe she has seen the light."

"Oh, she's always been a bit strange and I reckon she always will be. It happens when you lose your father suddenly. Remember Amy Jordan. A real hermit she was. We used to think she was a witch. Her father was murdered and her mother never recovered."

"I think the Jordans are related to the Robinsons", Mrs Wilson suggested, "and Marie's mother was related to some distant cousins too."

"You can't be too careful which family you marry into these days I'm sure."

"Well, I must be off or I'll never be done in time for dinner."

"Bye for now."

"See you tomorrow," joined in Mrs Wilson.

"Joan never seems to tire with the children dropping in with their families every day."

"Oh they have really done quite well for themselves don't you think? They have been able to set up all their seven children with farms."

"They did work very hard for a long time though. Maybe people have it too easy now."

At that moment Marie Robinson and the young man from Wanganui came out of the tea room. They were both smiling and said thank you in unison as they came to the counter. The young man paused and put the correct amount for the bill by the till.

"Thank you," said Mrs Baker, watching them walk lightly out onto the wet pavement.

"They seem so happy. I wonder what they are up to. I'm not sure that Miss Sinclair should mix with those two. I didn't have my glasses on. Did you see what the badge he was wearing said?"

"I think it said, 'Better Blatent Than Latent'. I wonder what . . ." Mrs Baker's eyebrows rose.

Miriam Saphira

A Market

Judy turned the VW into the driveway and stopped. Another day of work finished and we get paid tomorrow she thought. I can't wait for the weekend. I must look through the paper and see if there is something a bit more creative for me. If I have to work for my living I could at least have a satisfying job that offers some creative stimulation.

Judy ran up the steps tripping over a bone that Patch had left.

Damn Patch. Why can't she hide her bones like normal dogs do? I'm sick of tripping over bones, toys and dishes. "Patch! Patch!" Judy called out as she unlocked the door.

A muffled bark greeted her, as a black, white and brown patchwork dog leapt up with a purple sand-shoe in her mouth. Judy hugged her and gently removed the shoe.

"When will you start leaving our shoes and pick up your bones? Be a good girl and stop drooling over my clothes and let me make some tea. Now what will I have? I think I want some lemon tea to restore my sapphic sanity."

Judy plugged in the jug and went into the bathroom, kicking off her shoes as she went.

When the tea was made Judy carried it to the table and opened the newspaper. She glanced over the headlines; an earthquake in South America, wars, riots and espionage, nothing gay about newspapers.

Suddenly she had a thought. If ten per cent of the population was gay then five per cent of the news should be lesbian what with the Human Rights Commission and a fair deal for women. But where are the lesbians? If you look at this paper we don't exist. We're invisible.

Gay liberation happened in New Zealand in about 1971. Now fifteen years later what had lesbians got from it except each other? Sure there were lesbian counselling services in Auckland. The public knew we needed those to straighten our corkscrew minds. There was an alcohol abuse support group. The public knew we were all drunks. There was the soccer team and the public knew we were all butches who roamed the streets looking for femmes and we stole innocent wives from innocent husbands.

Swiftly Judy made a connection. It was little wonder that the public held such myths about lesbians when they never read any of the ordinary things about us.

There is nothing on television or in the Women's Weekly, or the free suburban papers. What lesbians need is a marketing strategy.

I can see it now, Judy thought. How to promote lesbians as okay people. Perhaps a documntary like the Aids doco the other night. Then a piece of fiction like "Dyke in The Family." Judy tried to think of a positive piece of fiction but all she could see was a family battle over the breakfast table, milk spilt over the toast, clumps of soggy weetbix abandoned on the Crown Lynn bowls and the air tense with wrangling.

"You need to settle down."

"You need a man."

"You need a good fuck."

"You need to wear decent dresses instead of those overalls."

"Oh, where did we go wrong?"

It must be possible to create good fiction when we've inherited Katherine Mansfield. Where is our New Zealand Patience and Sarah? Do we need a positive herstory to create fiction? After all it only needs to be realistic.

What about starting with an acceptable dyke? Marilyn Waring or Miriam Saphira. Now they look lesbian. The public know them, and they appear on television. Yeah, but they are both educated with uni degrees. Country dykes turned graduates, made it in the system. Now they have dropped out, or have they, if they write and things. They have dropped out of the patriarchal put-down anyway.

Judy scratched the top off her dermatitis scab and eased it along the strand of hair, inspected the brown and white scale with its fresh red bottom. It wasn't ready to be lifted. She flicked it off her knee.

Dykes were harder to market than I thought. Hey, there are Renee and Sandi Hall. They are well known. They could do with a bit more television coverage. We could make interesting things happen to them. A bison from the zoo in Sandi's back garden.

"Heroic Lesbian Writer Battles Bison."

Maybe a funny happening at the theatre. Let me see.

"Mercury Theatre overrun with lizards. Saved by nimble fingered lesbians and the show goes on."

We could have news stories around nurses and toll operators. I know lots of nurses. I can see background to the news stories.

"Did you know that lesbians stamp your letters, take your pulse and put your call through?"

Judy scratched her head again. I think I'd be better as a sub-editor than a news writer. I can't seem to get past the catchy headlines. It would be hard to keep the public's interest up for very long with these items. Of course five per cent of us would love the papers but that is hardly the numbers needed for a boom on the newspaper market.

Maybe advertising jingles would be better.

"Someone's Mum just doesn't know what someone's Mum really ought to know that someone's Mum better get to know that Lesbians are Lovely."

"Don't spend your days polishing the floor, spend those hours instead with the woman next door."

"Ask a lesbian for tea for that feel alive event for your tea-party or your dinner."

"There's more than one way to live and love. Lesbians are a real blessing to our society."

"Lesbians are fun, fun, fun . . ."

"Woof, woof!"

Judy's reverie was broken with Patch barking as she ran to the door. It was her flatmate Carol arriving home. Carol was cooking dinner tonight before they both headed out again for evening courses they were taking this year.

"Hi, Carol. Had a good day?"

"Oh, the usual snotty noses and hair pulling. Tony's mum was late again to pick him up. She goes to the hairdresser every Wednesday. She's worse than us."

"She must be depressed."

"Or insecure about her husband. She's such a nervous woman. I really feel sorry for her with those three young children. I don't really mind that much if she's late. She is always so apologetic. On other days she helps clean up. She really appreciates having kindy close by." Carol dropped her bag on the table and headed towards her room.

Now where was I? thought Judy, as she absentmindedly scratched her head again.

"Judy! Where's my hairbrush?"

"Dunno. Maybe under the handbasin. I think it fell down."

"Thanks, I've got it. Did you see the Times?"

Carol had this ability to keep up a shouting conversation wherever she was in the flat. Judy had always thought that it was because she was a kindergarten teacher and she was used to a certain level of clamour all day that she never noticed that she shouted for the first hour after she arrived home.

"What Times?" Judy felt a bit irritated. She was just starting to get into this idea of marketing.

Carol came back into the kitchen brushing her long blonde hair.

"The Sunday Times. There's an article about lesbians participating in the Women's Ministry. Seems they want our advice on job discrimination."

"Gosh, we've taken over the Government already. I knew I should have finished my degree."

Carol's eyebrows rose in surprise.

"I don't think they have actually let us hold the reins yet, let alone have any say."

"I'm sure we'll do it. I have just been having this vision. Just now, before you came in. Just think of it all."

"All what. What ever are you talking about?"

"Taking over the Government," Judy enthused as she went on.

"Think of all the work. There'll be lesbian departmental decisions, Select Dyke Committees, dyke dollars from the treasury, the health department supporting alternative medicines straight from our own witches, a Ministry of Dykes on Bikes, Lesbian Environmental Impact Reports and no more sprays . . . we may not need marketing strategies at all."

Fran Marno

Morgaine

I was born in Timaru in 1950, in a white working class family of Scottish and English ancestry. I have visited Scotland and loved it. All my life I have switched between writing and art but I am also interested in natural healing. I have done a course in herbal medicine and at present I am at Teachers' College training to be a secondary school art teacher. In Wellington I was involved in lesbian theatre, including the writing of short plays. I would like to organise a lesbian theatre group in Auckland and also a lesbian community arts festival. At the moment I am too busy playing part court jester part stroppy lesbian at Teachers' College.

Limbo

What an interminable time until I hear from you or see you again. Like being stretched on the rack, as I write in one of my letters to you.

I wrote my first letter two days after Maggie left, sitting on the bench in the herb garden in the feverish spring sun, hugging myself with remembered ecstasy, the sound the lust in my blood, mingling with birdsong and wind in the trees to make a wild, haunting music, the whole of my body etched in space as a passionate entreaty to her, revelling in this exquisite unrelenting torture.

— Dear Maggie, I wrote,

Seems ages since I said goodbye to you at the airport. I think of you all the time and miss you in my arms at night. Sorry for being so sloppy and sentimental — I get the feeling you dislike sentiment. My friends are all shaking their heads and saying — Typical Aries, falling in love at the drop of a hat. But what I feel for you is really special, as if I've known you for a long time. Maybe in some other life.

Apart from missing you life goes on as usual. The political scene is hotting up here with anti-lesbian legislation being debated in the House. It's already passed its first reading. The government is also talking again about cutting welfare spending another third which could mean total destitution for some wimmin unless we form working communities. Didn't you say wimmin on the coast had done that when they cut the unemployment benefit? We're having rallies every other night down at Parliament and outside the Town Hall about both debates. The White Right boys have been turning up too and we've been having quite violent confrontations. Ange and I both got into a scuffle the other night. Ange got a black eye. I bit one of them's hand almost to the bone to make him let go of her. Fortunately some other lesbians came to our defence. We were both badly shaken and angry. I think Ange's finding me a trial to live with (I keep haunting the letter box) but she's being very patient. Last night we went out to dinner and then to a play called Blacks Rule OK about Maori Sovereignty written by a young Maori womin still in her teens. It was excellent. Don't you miss having things like that to go to on the coast? Am looking forward to hearing from you. Please write soon or I'll wear out the path to the letter box. Lots and lots of love and hugs and kisses, Jess.

In the afternoon after posting the letter I was nagged by worrying thoughts of Maggie getting back with Helen, of Helen finding out she'd been with me. And she would go all out, of that I was sure, and try to get Maggie back. And Maggie would go, unable to see that she was being manipulated like a marionnette by Helen's mercilessly charismatic ego. A few days passed like this, alternating between bliss and excitement and anxiety and worry. At nights I would writhe in the aftermath of remembered passion but tried not to fantasise because fantasy is dangerous. It builds up expectations which cannot possibly be met.

Instead I try to imagine her life on the coast. I do this so well that sometimes I feel I'm on the coast with her, that only the ghost of myself is still in Wellington. At these times I'm wasted, at others larger than life with excitement at the thought of her.

I calculate it will take about four days for my letter to reach her. This means Monday at the earliest. By Friday the feeling of connecting with her had worn off a little. Life was beginning to reassume some aspect of normality. On Friday night I went to the club and danced and had a good time, thinking of her now and then, but enjoying the company of other wimmin, already with half of my mind, considering other romantic possibilities. Then a spasm of memory and for a moment the dance floor recedes and I see her for a brief second very clearly, more clearly than when I have been thinking of her for hours. Then it is gone again and either I hunt for it futilely or dance on regardless.

I'm aware that I'm obsessed and sometimes when I have no clear picture of Maggie in my head, which is most of the time these days, I wonder whether I'm simply in love with the idea of being in love and not with her at all. It's becoming so increasingly hard to visualise her. When I conjure up her image in my mind I get a jigsaw puzzle with all the pieces in the wrong place. There's a warning somewhere but I push it aside. Also, the sense I have of her as a womin, an identity, eludes me a lot of the time. I feel that in my obsession I'm in danger of losing her altogether. And sometimes I think — well I don't really know her at all, I've only just met her so why do I care?

Early Saturday morning Ange and I decided out of the blue to catch the ferry to Picton, stay the night in a motel, and travel back on the ferry the following day. Ange's a Gemini. We quite often decide to do spontaneous and madcap things like that. Which is why our friendship's such fun. We enjoy straight off the cuff unreasoned action. I remember the time we went to the Winter Show and ended up spending our kitty money.

— We won't go on any amusements, we'll just check out the lesbian visibility stall and look at the ghastly products.

That's what we said and ended up going on everything even the cake tin and the hydroslide which I enjoyed but Ange said it was like drowning and suffocating at the same time, and she wouldn't repeat the experiment even when I told her it was better on one's back. Another time which we're both terribly ashamed of, we went to the circus to protest at the mistreatment and abuse of animals and ended up watching the show. It's this kind of appetite for adventure and misdemeanour which makes me love Ange. She's also great to go graffitiing with. Owing to her almost supernatural acumen where police cars are concerned. We've never been caught yet.

So spontaneously deciding to go to Picton wasn't an unusual event. We packed a lunch to eat on the ferry, packed a few overnight things, and caught a taxi down to the ferry exactly half an hour before sailing time which was unusual for us. Unfortunately the seamen had been on strike so there was some debate as to whether the ferry would actually sail or not. As it was, even after we'd boarded, it was delayed for half an hour more during which time Ange and I bit our nails to the bone and Ange suddenly decided to give up giving up smoking. And then without warning the Wellington wharf began to recede and we were slipping through the intense calm blue of the harbour water. (It was a lovely day.) Ange and I having decided that going to Picton was the only thing we could possibly want to do, hugged each other with joy and relief that the adventure had begun.

We made ourselves comfortable on deck, me writing another letter to Maggie and Ange with a lusty lesbian novel which she kept distracting me with, by reading juicy bits out loud (several people sitting near us moved hastily away, one young girl seemed absolutely fascinated — there's a potential dyke for you I said to Ange). Perhaps because of my lack of concentration the letter to Maggie wasn't terribly successful:

Dear Maggie,

Am missing you terribly even though I'm enjoying myself right now. Ange and I are on our way to Picton for the weekend. We just decided to go this morning. Do you do off the cuff things like that?

Ange keeps distracting me by reading bits out of a very explicit lesbian novel. Even though my heart's full of you I'm finding it difficult to write. I was going to say I wish you were here but I don't know if that's strictly true because I'm really close to Ange and love spending time with her. It's strange how sometimes you feel so close and at other times I can't seem to feel any connection with you at all and the more I try the less I feel. I wonder if the times I do feel close are when you're thinking of me as well. At the moment it's as if I have no sense of you at all. I think that's why I'm writing this letter — to try and recapture you — but it isn't working. I haven't any news since the last letter, I don't know what's going to happen about the bookshop . . .

Here I interrupted the letter to ask Ange — What's going to happen about the bookshop. Ange looked guiltily up from her novel. — Don't know, Jess, the community can't afford to buy new premises and restock all in one go.

She frowned, made as if to speak, fidgeted. — Actually, Jess, I've been thinking, I might sell the house and start a new bookshop up.

The day had turned grey and cold around me. I stared at her bleakly. — But, Ange, you can't, I wailed. Where will we live?

— In a flat, like three quarters of lesbians do, Ange said somewhat aggressively and ungrammatically. Jess, you're always the one going on about privilege and owning property. We've had heaps of arguments over that. Or don't I count because I'm your friend and I'm giving you somewhere to live as well?

— But your grandmother left you that house, I protested miserably.

— Exactly, and how many lesbians have homes left to them by their grandmothers. I don't feel comfortable about it Jess.

You're providing a home for a working class womin, I said weakly.

You might come from a working class background, Jess, but I'd hardly call you working class now. You could buy your own house if you wanted to.

I gazed resentfully at Ange. I'd never suspected this goodygood aspect of her character.

— If you set up another bookshop, you'll mainly be benefitting middle class wimmin, I sneered. Why don't you run a health farm for the lesbian health collective and employ me as resident herbal doctor!

Ange looked at me sadly. — You really don't want me to sell the house, do you, Jess.

I huddled moodily, trying to mesmerise myself with the movement of the waves. Ange, you sell it over my dead body and your grandmother will turn in her grave. How long have you been thinking of it?

— Ages. The bookshop being burned just brought it all up again.

— But Ange, the fuckers could burn down the new one and then you'd have nothing.

— I still wouldn't be worse off than most dykes.

— I think if you want to do something you could buy up cheap flats and make them available to homeless dykes. If this new Social Welfare legislation goes through even a bookshop will be a luxury.

— That's a thought, what's happening with it?

— I think submissions close about the tenth. We should get our arses into gear and get one in. Honestly Ange, I wish you hadn't ruined my weekend by threatening me with homelessness.

Jess, you're melodramatic. We'll get a cosy little flat together. Try to be positive.

— You'll change your mind. You always do.

I abandoned my letter to Maggie and spent the rest of the ferry trip coming to terms with the idea of Ange selling the house and our moving into a flat. By the time we'd reached the Sounds I was feeling quite excited. Ange and I stood by the rail watching the blue water change to dark green as it touched the wooded land and talking enthusiastically about projects we could launch with her money. My feelings changed from resentment to love of Ange for having such marvellous ideas and I put my arm around her. — Lezzies, I heard someone whisper but when I turned round to glare it was hard to tell who'd said it.

By the time we reached Picton we were exhausted and the thought of finding a motel was a little daunting. After halfheartedly wandering up and down a few streets, making desultory enquiries and finding out that places were too expensive, we went to the Accommodation Centre and found ourselves a cheap, comfortable motel with a colour TV and spacious double bed. The manager seemed a bit nonplussed to encounter two wimmin coming from Wellington to stay the night and then going back the next morning so we let her think we were on some sort of sporting holiday.

— We should fuck all night so that part of it is true, I suggested. Ange looked shocked and we had another argument about using the word fuck to describe lesbian sex.

Looking back on that time spent with Ange in Picton I'm struck by how easy and totally stress free it was compared with the time I was to spend with Maggie later. We fitted into each other, flowed in and out of each other. Literally.

Because that night, propped up in bed with a cheap bottle of white wine, half a joint and a hilarious, grotesque "lesbian" horror film on telly we began to get physical with each other. What began as half hearted whimsical massaging of neck and shoulders became playful touching of breasts, stomachs. When Ange, still playful, put her hand between my legs, I groaned. Meaning, Ange don't do this. It'll wreck, our friendship. No do it, do it! Anyway Ange took it as a groan of desire and pretty soon I wasn't thinking — this shouldn't be happening, we're friends — I was writhing, gasping, wrapping myself round Ange like a live scarf, and, flung out of myself by the shock of orgasm, was immediately exploring the sleek purring mysteries of her, the secrets of her long-loved body, watching her eyes dilate with a sort of far away Geminian wildness the moment before she gave a long drawn shudder that echoed through my own body, and became limp and focused again in my arms. It had turned into a sporting holiday after all.

So we'd done it. We'd broken our taboo and rocketed our friendship out onto a perilous unknown planet. In the meantime we let it rest there. We curled into each other as we had often done before and went to sleep.

Fran Marno

Lynn Suttie

I am a feminist. I am Lesbian. I live in Auckland. I am a teacher.

To Be In Love With Other People

Jan recrosses her legs, sun warm on her back. She looks at her watch, unnecessarily; she has looked each minute for the last thirty.

"Where is he?" She stamps her crossed leg back to the ground, peering down the tree-lined road. Along the oak-lined park road advances a tall woman, wheeling a pushchair, coaxing a small child. Jan squirms, she's rather like David's wife.

"I'll wait five more minutes!"

The advancing woman drops her kit, its contents spilling. The child runs across the roadway — once all is retrieved the woman places the child in the pram; which promptly collapses.

"Who needs it?" murmurs Jan.

The woman stops by Jan.

"Do you mind if I sit here?"

After further glances at her watch Jan comments on the sleeping child. The woman asks the time, 2.35. The two women talk. Margaret, the mother, tells of her trip to Auckland; she is staying with her parents.

"Are you waiting for someone?" asks Margaret, Jan nods.

"He's late!"

The two women discuss man's fallibility, wearily they sigh. Jan replies that, yes, he's someone special, but he works hard, has so many commitments it is difficult for them to have time together. Margaret smiles, she's come to Auckland to think things through. Her husband has always worked hard, they've not had much time together, now he's having an affair!

A car drives up, Jan leaps up angry! David holds up a hand to stop her.

"I've only got five minutes. Came to say, sorry, I can't see you today. Sorry."

As she sits, Margaret says, "I know I shouldn't . . ."

"Don't," snaps Jan. If she talks she will cry.

"Would you like a coffee?"

They walk up to the kiosk, neither woman wanting to leave, both thinking of the scene, its meaning to them.

"He's married."

Margaret glances at the flamboyantly dressed woman. Her initial distress at the encounter has softened to allow compassion for this vulnerable young woman.

The two women sit opposite, for the first time they face each other; eyes mirrored.

32 Rose Avenue
Kelburn
Christchurch
27 March.

Dear dear Jan.

This Easter holiday finds me surrounded by in-laws, John and the children; thank heavens Mum and Dad stayed in Auckland.

I have thought and thought about my time in Auckland so much. I keep smiling to myself, "the cat that got the cream"; then it really hits! That day in the park my emotions raged in ways I'd never known. Please try to understand why I had to come back — John and the children need each other. I can't cut those ties. He wanted to try again, we've been over this!

My coming back here is NOT a denial of what happened between you and me. I'm not ready to throw away all my life has been.

Please change your mind, come for the holidays. The children will be with their grandparents and then we can talk. I'll be free every day.

Write soon!

Margaret.

45 Kikorangi Road
Grey Lynn
Auckland
1st May.

Dear Marg.

School's HELL! The flat is HELL! My car has broken down! The only thing that keeps me going is that the holidays are nearly here. No, I won't come to Chch. I'm going to sleep in, read and buy my winter wardrobe (couple of new op-shops down the road). I might even look for an all-women flat.

I've been going to "Feminist Teachers." I can't stop seeing and feeling all the shit women have had to put up with. The consciousness-raising really runs away with you, once you get started.

You should look for a women's group; read "The Women's Room" by Marilyn French (it'll do you good).

Thanks for the photos — but don't send any that have him in! I've cut him out.

You could come up here while the kids are away?

Love Jan.

5 May

Dear Marg,

I never quite believed it was you when I answered the phone. Then to hear your voice saying "Let's meet in Wellington!" You are a wonderful, wonderful woman. Brave too!

I can hardly bear the wait.

Jan

9 May

Dearest Jan,

I am very sorry I won't be able to meet you in Wellington. I had a big talk to John, about us. He said it was disgusting! I had to choose, him and the children. I'm not brave. I can't risk my children.

Please forgive me. It seems I've been hurting you since we met. There is so much to say but I will have to trust you can believe how special loving you has been.

I'm sorry it's turned out like this!

Margaret

". . . and that's how it was. I often wonder how she is. I'd like to write but don't think I should."

Clara nodded. As Jan spoke she tried to recall how she had been when she and Margaret had met. Clara sat with Jan, her expression intent, oblivious to the hustle in the bar.

When they met Jan had made mention of a special woman. Clara in her usual way had left the remark, Jan realised, until she was ready for a full telling.

"What would you say?"

I want to tell her that I do understand although it hurt. Together we were powerful, without meeting her I would not be as I am. Strong, happy. I want for her to have that too. I hate to think of her in that life. A marriage where it is expected that she gives all her energy.

I want to tell her about my life. My dreams, the women who are my family, you!

When they first danced, then talked Jan had felt herself smile and smile. She felt the stirrings of intrigue. Her eyes seeking constant contact yet feeling embarrassed if she found Clara looking at her. She was too aware of Clara's presence. She did not need to give energy into another relationship. Her life was full. Her work fulfilling, she worked long and hard. The caring and support from her friends filled the gaps she had been unaware of until Margaret and the subsequent void.

The intimate relationships since had been thrilling but without depth and painful to leave. Yet she kept recalling all she had been told about Clara. Imagining how she looked. Scheming on how to see her again, how to have time to talk to her.

Now, having spent the day summoning the courage to phone her, here they were! How had she ended up talking about Margaret? They had begun talking of the recent Reform Bill, what that time had meant to them. From there they talked of women's wisdom. So many women hearing the decades of scoffing at "intuition" had let their wisdom fade. Jan's rational-self was fighting a battle with her wisdom.

"Yes, this woman is amazing, she hears, understands. We can laugh together! She challenges me! But . . ."

"Do you have the time for this, a new relationship? You always get too involved!"

Clara took Jan by the hand. They moved to the dance floor, their shoulders rocking to the beat of the loud music. As they danced they made contact, eye, hand. Their shoulders and hips brushing as their bodies moved in unison with the music and each other.

"I want to wake up next to you . . ." began the next, slower song. Clara and Jan held each other, thigh to thigh, pelvis and breast. As they brought their heads together each felt the hair of the other. Their perceptions heightened so they felt each strand, mingling and drawing across cheek and skin. Their bodies melded.

Jan as she looked about saw many women. All proud, feeling good; at one with body, clothing, psyche. Jan felt a surge of confidence. Almost she felt, arrogance. She, these women belonged! They knew what they needed.

Clara stroked her finger down from Jan's cheek, across her lips and down her throat. The cool finger on her sweat-damp skin caused a sharp sensation. Of its own accord Jan's body leant to the hand.

They left. As they drove they were silent. Each in private thought, although aware of the presence of the other and the space between them. Jan stopped the car. The scene before them; silvered water, glass smooth. The further sea a solid blackness as the cloud cover shut out the full moon. The flashing lights across the harbour (Clara counted six), were flashing independently, without an attempt at unison. The glitter of city lights and refracted moonlight allowed the two women to see. The shadows that fell across their faces, a protection from their new found exposure and vulnerability with each other.

"I . . ."

Clara placed her fingertips on Jan's lips to quiet her. Of their own accord Jan's lips kissed the fingers. Clara leant over with her hand resting against Jan's throat, her lips brushed across Jan's mouth. The two women held each other still. Their fingers stroking, their kisses fleeting as they moved, hair stroking skin.

Clara opened the car and they climbed out into the fresh earth. The dew-damp grass made Jan's feet hum. They walked.

"We need go only as far as we like. It's enough to be this close." Jan stroked Clara's hair, interweaving it through her fingers, drawing it across her palms. She lent and kissed the woman who so calmly moved her inner being.

The two women embraced. Jan's arms anchored on Clara's hips, Clara's on Jan's shoulders.

As the days and weeks became months, the women talked; of dreams, past, families, work. They shared beach walks, jam making, picnics, movies, wallpapering.

When the letter arrived Jan noted it had been redirected from Kikorangi Street. The hand writing seemed familiar. As she began reading her breath all but ceased.

32 Rose Avenue
Kelburn
Christchurch
12 June.

Dear Jan,

I will be in Auckland soon and would like to see you. I has been difficult not to communicate, I thought letters would be inert. Write if I should call when I arrive.

Love Margaret

It was now the end of July, the letter had lain at the flat. Jan looked up the number and dialled.

"I'd like to leave a message for Margaret when she comes . . ."

"Jan it's me. I'm so pleased you phoned. How are you? Can I see you?"

Now Margaret was due, Jan felt her initial thrill wane. Perhaps they should have arranged a neutral meeting place. Margaret may find Clara an intrusion. Clara said she would leave after they had eaten. How to say it all? What did she intend by renewing contact?

As Margaret walked towards the gate she wondered at her reactions. Her body was surreal in its tranquility. Her eyes felt huge, their peripheral vision extended.

Could Jan be angry? She had not been able to detect any emotion from their brief call.

Meeting Clara was a shock. Her image of Jan had been held from the last time together. She had not prepared herself for this. Some of the subtle changes were apparent. Gone were the flashy, slightly revealing clothes. Replaced by strong coloured, cotton trousers and loose shirt. Her hair was cut in various levels, the front stood up aggressively. Her earrings were large triangles of paua. Clara was in similar clothing but each woman was unique within the style.

As they ate Margaret and Jan looked fleetingly at each other. By turn, explaining to Clara how they had met. Neither mentioning the last letter. Margaret knew Clara would know. They talked of the children. Then of how Clara and Jan had met, the house that Jan and Clara now shared.

Margaret sat and surveyed the room in which she waited. Jan's returning footsteps, Margaret's deep indrawn breath and following sigh stirred the pall of silence. Jan gathered the plates. Margaret drained her coffee. Neither looked at the other. As Margaret stood her chair scraped harshly. Jan swung around. The tears held within her eyes. They clutched, elbows knocking. Their embrace symmetrical in stance and emotion.

The assurance each had projected in Clara's presence now gone, no longer necessary.

"I believe one gets to think being 'in love' less and less important, but loving people never gets less important, and you are one of those people I love most, as you know well, and however much either you or I may happen to be in love with other people my real feeling for you doesn't change."   *Vanessa Bell*

Not a Sad Ending

Shit! She woke knowing by the dry sulphurous taste in her mouth, the scratchy sensation in her chest and throat, that the cold she had been too busy to have, had taken hold. In the silence of her flat she tested her voice, croaky!

THROAT: Avenue of expression, channel of creativity. Swallowed anger. The inability to speak for oneself.

The metaphysical cause did nothing to cheer her. Since meeting the woman she had tried to keep cool, just bodily reaction. The woman dynamic, strong, powerful yet repressed, searching, defensive. She didn't lack the ability to speak, they had talked for hours. How to make her understand, believe that what she offered was possible, their bond could enhance their self-less lives.

A lover who loved her because of the woman she was. A woman with a partner, a "marriage", family. A woman who devoted her life to women. Helen was offering friendship, not a replacement from one coupling to another. Was the price of the woman's life to be the denial of any affinity with others?

The women's stories were links, shared bonds. Both had offered their limitations, attractions honestly, maturely; which didn't help much now she had fallen in love! Their kisses, lip-brushes so gentle, thrilling. The woman's body, sleek, her eyes, their glances, many-folded messages.

As she lay the scenes unfolded in her mind. They had sighted each other two years previously. Helen had arrived at morning tea, the woman, her cropped hair, body rigidly relaxed, legs thrust out defiant in the room of chattering women workers. Helen's eye kept tracking back to her. The bell rang, the woman rose, shoulders high, hands pocketed, she strode out. Three weeks later Helen began work; the woman had left. Now she pondered that first time, neither had spoken nor acknowledged the other yet she knew both had been aware.

They stood on the jetty shivering watching the moon, hearing the quiet talk of the fishing men. Not touching, sleeves brushing. Helen's trembling remained deep within, the woman appearing calm and nonchalant. Once more neither had spoken nor acknowledged the feelings that were within. They had parted with words of how great it was to talk.

If it had ended there she would not be in this state now! Blocked ears, sinus, tearful.

SINUS: Irritation to one person, someone close.

Well she knew who that was! She thumped her pillow, got up, her flat was full of memories.

They had exchanged poems; touch me, kiss me poems. They shared dinners and the kisses had begun. Their lovemaking overwhelmed them. Fine-boned angular fit to comfortable softness. The tastes and smell of their sex.

As the woman left, Helen watched her walk away, hands pocketed, shoulders high. Not so cool any more, girls!

Three hours, more talking on the phone. What did it mean? The woman knew Helen knew. As she moved through her Sunday, coffee, washing, vacuuming. No telephone calls. Helen thumped angrily. No space for her. A woman on her own intruding into a life seemingly full, highlighting needs, a risk too great!

I care, said the woman, but I have little time to give. I have responsibilities, you have touched me. My time with you is important to me and I will not throw it away. I will sort it out. We will be friends but it can't be more.

Helen felt the distancing, needed it, enhanced it. The woman would not, could not call. Helen was surrounded by the depression of a love just tasted; solitary grieving.

She would not be guilty. Since meeting Helen, since spending time and caring for her she had made her position clear, even when unclear in her own mind. Helen accused her of mixed messages; well the feelings were mixed! What she said was true, what she did was how she felt!

On this hazy Sunday she knew Helen would want her to call. They had tripped into emotions neither of them were prepared for: gaps and passion they had aroused each in the other.

As she walked, her feet striking the pavement, she let the resentment flow over her. Helen had no commitments, she could do as she pleased. She breezed in with her patient listening, warm body all too eager, assurances of handling the confines of their relationship. Now, the emotional balance had swung too far.

Chewing a grass stem, elbows propping her body, the outer pose calm and relaxed. Inwardly her stomach churning. What Helen was asking seemed so possible. To love, care, would add to her life. A new relationship that would neither take from nor negate her. Something special just for her! Yet she knew to continue their quiet talks; that the close feelings would sweep over them. More time, more touching, more energy; she didn't have it to give but the vacuum was a rushing biting wind.

The woman and Helen moved through their Sunday, each a vessel of mixed emotion. Each yearning for contact. Their simultaneous thoughts hurt. Both wishing away the pain. The delight in their intimacy hastily put aside. The deep sorrow that to never touch or meet was the comfortable, the only solution for the woman.

In future time they may think of the other. Remembering times shared, wondering of the other. A calm resoluteness, selfless caring for the intimacy they once shared that they gave as a sacrifice.

Fran Marno

Barb Abernethy

I was born at a very early age, suffered a happy childhood, married, had a daughter, divorced, came out, survived heady, hefty, miraculous affairs, a long eager relationship with booze, another reluctant relationship with skin cancer; then gained some sense and moved to Mac Bay with daughter to live with 'The Dyke'.

I go on writing and surviving in a non-violent, drug and alcohol free environment; dreaming of a clean and sober dyke community.

Evensong

I stepped off the train and searched easily amongst the many faces for Ruth. Not being able to locate her didn't upset me. My little sister rarely made an appearance anywhere on time. One grew used to her turning up some ten minutes after everyone else.

I let the crowd thin out around me and then walked over to one of the old wooden benches the railways had provided for transient passengers and the like. Putting my pack down beside me, I lit a cigarette and resigned myself to the wait.

Most of the crowd had disappeared. A few station employees wandered around here and there, making feeble attempts to look busy. One or two lost souls seemed to be waiting, as I was. But nobody took much notice of anybody else — and that was the way I liked it.

I'd finished my cigarette when I spotted the womyn. At first I took little notice of her as she approached the only other young womyn — apart from myself — on the platform. With one quick glance I considered her to be the conservative type, dressed as she was in a brown, tweed skirt-suit, with matching, made-to-last, walking brogues. Blending perfectly with these, a brown fedora clung to her shortish, curly, black hair. Wrapped around the collar of her buttoned-to-the-neck, snow-white blouse she wore a bright, lipstick-red, satin scarf with amazing casualness. The scarf seemed incongruous at first glance, but with a little reflection one could see it as a subtle addition to her outfit.

I glanced at my watch, wondering where on earth Ruth was, and lifted my head up to find the womyn standing squarely in front of me.

"Evensong?" she hesitated, probably feeling quite silly using such a stupid name. I know I would have felt slightly absurd. Her voice drifted over me like a leaf floating on a breeze.

With a contained chuckle, I nodded affirmation and corrected her. "Eve Ensaghn," I smiled, softening the correction.

"Oh!" she looked somewhat startled — for a moment so brief one could've missed it. "Oh, I am sorry. The connection was dreadful when Ruth called. I'm here to get you there. Sorry to have kept you waiting, but Ruth's not the best with visual descriptions, so I thought I'd wait until the mob dispersed."

Her confidence was slightly overwhelming and had me subconsciously catching my breath. I made a fumbling grab for my pack and tried to stand, all in one go. That got me as far as getting my foot caught in a stray strap and almost falling against her.

The gentle touch of her hand on my bare arm had me even more breathless as she reached out to help me. With one graceful step she had picked up my pack and had me standing squarely on my feet again.

I took the proffered pack, threw it over my right shoulder, and trotted dutifully along beside her as she led the way to her car.

The road to Ruth's cottage seemed hellishly long that day. I sat, tensed up inside, as close to the door as I could, trying not to seem hopelessly reserved. I doubt that she even noticed. She seemed to be away in her own little world somewhere.

Having put my trust in this womyn, having not once doubted that she would get me to Ruth, I now realised I didn't even know her name. Her self-introduction had been overlooked along the way. Apart from knowing she was a very classy dresser who drove the very latest model Sierra, I knew absolutely nothing about her. It all seemed vaguely crazy. I didn't even know how she fitted into Ruth's world.

I tried to sit back and relax while she drove on, her expertise behind the wheel rarely found in the average driver. As much as I wanted to, I dared not smoke. The ashtray on the dashboard was obviously more useful to her as a storage compartment for paperclips, thumbtacks, and other such small objects.

So I sat, fidgeting with my fingers, and wishing time away so I could step into Ruth's lounge, throw myself down on her lumpy, old, beloved, Chesterfield couch and light up.

We twisted around a sharp bend in the road and my chauffeur spun across the gravel surface to avoid the sheep and her two offspring racing madly in all directions at the sight of the car. I could see it happening before it did — us hitting the small embankment on the side of the road and flipping over. I closed my eyes, wishing the image away, and then realised that we were still moving along at a regular pace.

God herself knew how, but that womyn had managed to avoid the sheep and drive on as though she encountered such obstacles every day. I really had to look at her with admiration.

"Okay?" The question was another drifting leaf. The look, one of genuine concern.

"Fine," I lied through my teeth, managing a wan smile, and automatically reached for my cigarettes before remembering the ashtray.

My inadvertant action didn't go unnoticed. As deftly as she must have pulled away from those sheep, she now swept the car over to the side of the road and stopped.

"If you must, please . . ." she reached across me to open the door and placed my packet of cigarettes in my hand. There was no hint of annoyance in her voice. She just seemed to understand my need of the moment.

I stepped out of the car and walked a little distance away from it. I didn't want her to think I was uncouth enough to expect her to breathe my smoke. A tall poplar tree made a good backrest and I leaned against it while I smoked. Some of my previous reserve seemed to be melting away because of her easy manner. I was actually beginning to feel more comfortable with her.

Even after I'd finished my cigarette I made no move to return to the car. I let my thoughts wander on and had almost forgotten our purpose for being on the road when there was a gentle touch on my shoulder.

"Ready to go?"

I reddened, hoping she didn't have the ability to read each and every one of my thoughts. I didn't want her to know — yet — that I had been imagining myself in bed with her. Sometimes such crazy images just swept into my head, unbidden.

We walked back to the car side by side to continue our journey.

It was no real surprise to see Ruth lounging about in her old wicker chair on the front porch when we pulled up in front of her cottage. I threw her a cheerful wave, spun round to retrieve my pack from the back seat of the car, and stepped out.

I was almost on the porch myself when I realised that Ruth had propped herself up on crutches to make her way towards me. Her right leg was in a plaster-cast from her heel to just above her knee.

"Cartilage," she grinned easily at my disturbed look as she explained. "Finally braved the odds and had it attended to. Thought I'd surprise you."

"You succeeded," I hugged and kissed her soundly. "But then, you have a habit of succeeding with your surprises," I added meaningfully, nodding furtively towards the back of the Sierra where my escort was busy pulling various objects out of the trunk.

"Do give the poor Doctor a hand, Evie darling", Ruth chuckled. "I'm not much flamin' help to anyone in this damned dancing pump."

I shut my mouth even more quickly than it had dropped open, hoping Ruth wouldn't notice my astonished response to her information. 'Doctor' is it? I thought, turning back down the steps towards the car. Oh well, at least I can now call her something, even if it is only 'Doc.'

I'm still not sure which one of us ordered Ruth back to her chair, but she was still sitting there looking sullen when we had finished unloading the car. I suggested taking a break from activities for a cuppa.

"I'll get it," Ruth blurted out eagerly, looking akin to a hippopotamus wallowing around in the mud as she tried to jump to her feet.

"Oh Ruth, sweetheart", I laughed with her when she thumped back down in her chair with a wallop. "Stay where you are. I'm quite capable of making a pot of tea."

"Mmmm? Well, I guess it only takes one — so I think I'll go and change these dreadful clothes."

I watched the good Doctor disappear and threw a questioning look at Ruth. When she merely winked back at me I almost backhanded her across the arm.

"Okay, Ruth. Give," I demanded affectionately.

"Give what?" Ruth was thoroughly enjoying herself, keeping me in suspense.

"Give with the info. I want to know as much as you do about that womyn, and how she fits into your life."

"Name, rank and serial number, eh?"

"Something like that. So get on with it."

Ruth chuckled, gave me a few brief details, and then told me to go make the tea before her other guest reappeared on the porch.

At the sound of Doctor Amelia Thorne's step onto the porch I glanced up from our chatter and caught my breath yet again because of her. The change was incredible. She now wore a very baggy, cool, cotton t-shirt, and skimpy cotton shorts — both garments whiter than white. I suspected that was all she wore as I looked at her, and reddened as my imagination took off all by itself again.

I figured it was just as well that Ruth was such an avid chatterbox Amelia really didn't have time to notice me, because my thoughts were going crazy. I was sure my face turned red every time I couldn't resist glancing furtively in her direction. Suddenly it didn't seem like such a great idea to spend the weekend with my little sister. I just wanted to disappear until Doctor Thorne had taken her leave.

I put my empty mug down beside the chair I was sitting on. The very next time my two companions were so engrossed in their conversation that they wouldn't notice what I was up to, I shoved my cigarettes and lighter into my pocket and slipped away.

I had a helluva lot of thinking to do — alone — and I knew just the place to do it.

I spread myself comfortably down on the soft, warm, grassy ground with my back propped up against the trunk of a fallen oak tree. I closed my eyes and willed myself to think straight. What was I going to do? I'd only known the womyn a matter of hours and here I was, already imagining making room in my life for her. It was crazy. *I* was crazy. The whole damned *world* was crazy. It really was all just a bit too much.

Doctor Amelia Thorne was really getting under my skin, and she didn't even know it. Or did she? Every time she came near me she gave me the impression that she knew *exactly* what she was doing to me. I felt she could read my every thought, relate to my every emotion, *knew* my every feeling. And still those crazy images kept flashing through my head. I seemed to be unable to do anything about it. My only possible course, at least until I had sorted myself out, was to avoid her.

But even that was impossible.

I opened my eyes and there she was, walking into the clearing from along the very same track I had used. She walked gently, slowly, with the barest of discernable swaggers.

Oh, yes! She knew damned well what effect she had on me all right. I could see it in her eyes as she advanced directly towards me with a small, teasing, smile. She continued, obviously filled with intention, ever closer to my frozen form. She stopped at my feet, looking down on me with easy confidence.

We didn't speak. I didn't move. I watched as she dropped to her knees, placing one either side of my legs. She reached forward to caress my cheek with a feather-light touch. Then she put both hands out, one either side of my head, against the tree trunk.

All movement ceased for the most fleeting moment.

"Evensong," she whispered on the breeze, and for the very first time ever I liked the name.

Her kiss, at first warm, soft, gentle, was soon one of question, her tongue gently prising my lips apart, then probing, pushing, exploring, asking.

This can't be happening, I thought, undecided as to her intentions. And I can't let it happen. Not now. Not like this.

In an instant I pulled away, hitting my head rather harshly against the tree trunk — and woke up.

Fran Marno

Mil Gibson

I lack spontaneity in relating to bigots, homophobics, psychiatrists and racists, but apart from that I like most people. I am vegetarian and think animals are human. I live in Christchurch where the easterly blows and love my partner and my kids.

The Time is Now

There was no way she would ever enter into another relationship. When Lauren had died that was the end.

The last five years had been lonely, and she could not deny that. Would there be still twenty, thirty lonely years ahead? She could live to be seventy, or eighty, with her rotten luck.

But would she have enough mental and emotional strength to live out that long on her own? Apart from suicide she would have no choice.

Damnation! — How long time was! The only time when time was short was when you wanted it to be long. What a contradiction life was.

She glanced down at her watch. Ten forty-five. Should she go home now or should she stay?

There it was again! Time! One of these days she was going to go away somewhere — maybe rent a house in the country — somewhere where there was no radio, no television or newspapers, and she would leave her watch at home and hide all the clocks (if the house had any) and she would live by her feelings. Eat when hungry, sleep when sleepy. All the time — or no time — in the world. But then it might be a bit like existing in a vacuum, just herself for herself. Would she be enough for her? Not if she kept thinking the way she was thinking now.

Why was she sitting here depressing herself like this? Perhaps it was the couple of drinks she'd had. After all, alcohol was a depressant.

Everyone seemed to be having a lot of fun. Except her, of course; sitting in a too-low chair against the wall, almost blending in with the grey-fawn wallpaper behind her, pregnant with self-pity. Jeez, it was a wonder that it wasn't burned into the wall in flaming neon above her head: THIS WOMAN IS TOTALLY ENGROSSED IN HER OWN SICKENING SELF-PITY. DO NOT TOUCH. DO NOT APPROACH.

Perhaps another drink would pep her up? But was it worth pushing through the jumbling, dancing, tangled figures crowding the small room to get something that was probably only going to keep her toilet-trotting half the night?

At last, someone changed the tapes. Music was amazingly evocative. This music had a beat she could understand, a rhythm she could dance to. Music could enter the blood like a virus, sending the senses spiralling, or deep into melancholy. Like most lovers, she and Lauren had had their meaningful music and secret songs; songs that, over the years she had watched others dance to at parties such as this, while she, hiding the grief that memory brought, had stood quietly aside until the waves of desolation and longing had receded. No, time never healed, it just gave you the distance to adjust, accept. Now she could hear those songs, listen to the music they had once shared, and not feel the searing pain any more. She had learned that grief; true, aching missing-that-person grief was, in its way, an acknowledgement of the love you had for that person. That you did love and that it didn't die when the person you loved died.

Someone — who thought she should enter into another relationship — had once accused her of holding morbidly to the past. She, in return, had tried to explain that at first Lauren's death, to her, had seemed like the end of everything but when, later, she began to pick up the torn threads of her life and knit them together again she simply found out that she quite liked her own company and that it was not her love for Lauren that stopped her from seeking love again — although initially, and with honesty, she had to admit to an emotional battle with a complex mixture of loyalty and grief — but then, growing accustomed to her own ways, settling into her own routines, she didn't want to have to summon up the necessary mental energy to change it all again.

So for her, when Lauren died, that was the end. Besides, she wasn't lonely all the time. Summer evenings, when the fragrance of flowers and freshly cut grass hung heavy on the warm, still air, and the wide sky was ribboned with sunset pinks and dusky lilac-blue, and there was no-one to share it with; the perfume of spring blossom; the smell of sudden raindrops splashing flatly down onto hot pavements; winter cold when there was no-one to curl up close to; after meetings or parties when there was no-one to talk it over with . . . well, those were lonely times. But, by and large, being with herself was something she could accommodate.

Not that her own company was that likeable tonight.

She looked again down at her watch. Eleven-fifteen. The room was even more crowded now. Late-comers pushing in through the hot, noisy movement of the dancing figures.

This was no good, this lonely introspection. Nor was it her usual way. There would be coffee going out in the kitchen. Also, if she knew women's parties, some stimulating discussion. Some of the best discussions she had ever entered into had been held, spontaneously, in the kitchen at lesbian women's parties.

She stood up and made her way through the crowd and out into the small kitchen. Once there it was like witnessing an attempt at a Guiness record-book effort to see how many women could be crowded into seven feet of room space. Laughing, jostling across each other for coffee or milk, talking animatedly, there were at least three different discussions taking place.

"Anna will know!" someone shouted, as she pushed her way into the room. "Hey, Ann, wasn't it Leonore Grace who wrote Strong Women and Free?"

She shook her head. "Sorry, Jean, it was Petra Grace."

A loud ooh went up at her reply.

"Well, I knew it was something Grace," the first speaker defended herself above the joking calls and laughter.

She squeezed her body through the others', finally making it to the bench now covered with used glasses, cups with dregs of cold coffee or tea settling brownly in their bottoms, and the remnants of pastry rolls and crunched up chip bags. She pushed aside a half-eaten sandwich, an apple core and an empty Just Juice carton in her search for a clean cup. There was none so she pushed her sleeves up, almost to her elbows, cleared a space in the bench sink and began to run hot water into it as she emptied the dregs from the cups and dropped the accumulated left-overs into a large brown paper bag someone had conveniently discarded nearby.

It was a crush, doing dishes in such a confined space, and she had just finished wiping the last of the glasses when one of the two women who had thrown the party pushed in beside her, mildly chastising her for cleaning up, but thanking her all the same, before being swallowed up again into the crowd behind them.

Her hands dried, everything tidy on the bench — awaiting the next onslaught — she leaned back against the wall and slowly sipped a hot freshly made cup of coffee as she watched and listened to the surge of women in the tiny room. As some left to rejoin the dancing in the other room others took their place. It was a women-kaleidoscope of movement and sound, and in some strangely objective way she felt both a part of it and apart from it. At least she wasn't feeling so down now.

There was a sudden movement and pushing at the outside door leading into the room and a laughing noisy group entered, the women inside pressing together to let them in. Four were women that she knew by sight but the last one in, dark, a head taller than the others, was a stranger to her. There was about her, from what Anna could see, an air of quiet confidence. Nothing patronising or superior, but a certain appealing calmness. And her eyes — large and darkly hazel, slowly took in the scene before her with that same appealing calmness.

Anna studied her face, as she stood there looking out over the crowd, until those large, dark eyes met hers and held her gaze for long moments . . .

Seemingly endless, deeply significant moments, and even when someone spoke to her, and she answered them, her eyes never left Anna's, until, finally, the sheer pressure of the crowd around her forced her to move out and into the other room.

Anna stayed where she was, pressed back against the wall, her coffee cup still held in her hand, and she was trembling — actually trembling. Not a physical hand-shaking, knee-knocking trembling but an inner exciting gut tremor, an almost forgotten whammy tightening somewhere behind her solar plexus and a feeling of light-headedness.

Jeez! What was wrong with her! First depression then tiredness. That's what it must be! She was feeling quite flakey, actually. Again, another check with time. Twelve-thirty. She should probably quietly leave now. The party had become even more boisterous and no-one would notice if she slipped away.

But those eyes — That look —

Of course, she didn't have to go yet. There was no-one waiting for her — only the empty house, the ticking of the clock and the dripping of the taps.

But what if she stayed? Was there any point? She had hardly been an active participant during the evening — neither giving nor receiving, which was her own stupid fault. Yet she wasn't normally a social bump on a log so how come she had managed to let herself slip into such a bummer mood?

Perhaps she had better go before she regressed completely!

Looking into the maze of bodies in the other room she decided it would be easier to go out the back door and around through the front to get her jacket and car keys, which she had left in the front bedroom.

It was warm and softly moonlit outside as she picked her way under the tangle of shrubs and bushes lining the path to the front of the house. She moved quietly up the front steps and over the wide wooden verandah and was about to open the panelled front door when someone pulled it open from the inside. She pulled back a little to make room for whoever was coming out and looked straight into a pair of darkly hazel eyes.

"Hullo," the other woman said, "you must have read my mind. I was just coming around to see you. Thought it would be easier this way than pushing through the crowd."'

Anna's sudden intake of breath seemed to stay caught in her throat while a bird began crazily beating its wings somewhere behind her midriff.

"Weren't going, were you?" the other woman asked. Her voice was warm and deep. "Least I hope not. Not before we get to know each other."

Her eyes — those eyes — seemed to absorb Anna's very being.

"Well?" she laid a cool hand on Anna's arm, the electricity of the contact sending a tingling through Anna's body.

"No, — I — "

"Are you with someone? Or do you have to meet someone?" the other woman questioned.

"No, — I — " Anna gave a sudden laugh, drawing her gaze away from the other woman's. "No, — I'm sorry, I'm not usually as stupid sounding as this."

It was the other woman's turn to give a low, gentle laugh. "I'm sure no-one could accuse you of being stupid," she said, looking directly into Anna's face. "But I also don't want to intrude —"

"No, no," Anna said, quickly. "There's no intrusion. I mean, I'm on my own. That is — well, I'm always on my own —" Really! Now she WAS sounding quite stupid.

The other woman gave a relieved sigh. "Thank heavens, then, — I was a bit worried in case —" she left the sentence unfinished but the pressure of her hand on Anna's arm gently increased. "Look, if you don't want to go back inside we could sit out here for a while. Would you mind?"

Anna shook her head. "No. I mean yes. Yes, of course. That would be nice."

Nice?! What was wrong with her? She was sounding like the original village idiot. Of course she would like to sit out there, with her. She would LOVE to sit out there. She couldn't think of anything she would like to do more than sit out there — with her.

The trembling within her had now travelled down to her knees and she was almost grateful to be able to sit down.

Every one of her senses was alive to the touch and presence of the woman beside her. The very air around them seemed to pulse and vibrate with the awareness of their being.

"My name is Gillian. I am unattached, and I want to be with you."

The simple statement was spoken in a low, even voice.

They sat in silence for a long time, neither woman moving but looking out into the darkened garden in front of them. Finally, moving her hand to cover Anna's where it gripped the edge of the verandah, Gillian turned and looked at her. "Don't ask me why, or how, or expect me to explain it. I don't know what happens, or how it happens, or even quite what happens. I just know that that's the way it is and that's the way I want it to be. And I feel that that's the way it is for you, too."

Anna loosened her grip on the verandah edge and turned her hand up to press, curling, around into Gillian's.

"It's a funny thing, time —" she mused, softly, then turning, full faced, she smiled gently into Gillian's eyes. "And my name's Anna," she said, "and I would very much like to be with you."

Footsteps sounded, padding along beside the house as two figures hurried out to the front gate and their parked car. They never looked back or saw the couple sitting close together in the warm dark on the verandah edge, and Anna, listening to the echo of the car engine as they drove away gently released her hand from Gillian's long enough to remove the watch from her wrist and carefully drop it into her pocket.